Christmas
Camp
Wedding

By Karen Schaler

Fiction
Christmas Camp Wedding
Christmas Camp

Non-Fiction
Travel Therapy: Where Do You Need to Go?

Christmas Camp Wedding

A NOVELLA

KAREN SCHALER

WM

WILLIAM MORROW IMPULSE

An Imprint of HarperCollins*Publishers*

CHRISTMAS CAMP WEDDING. Copyright © 2019 by Karen Schaler. All rights reserved. Printed in the United States of America. No part of this book may be used or reproduced in any manner whatsoever without written permission except in the case of brief quotations embodied in critical articles and reviews. For information, address HarperCollins Publishers, 195 Broadway, New York, NY 10007.

Digital Edition JANUARY 2019 ISBN: 978-0-06-288447-3
Print Edition ISBN: 978-0-06-288453-4

Cover design by Amy Halperin
Cover photographs © AnnaGodfrey/istock/Getty Images (roses);
Dumitrita Albu/Christin Lola/Shutterstock (2 images)

William Morrow Impulse is a trademark of HarperCollins Publishers.

William Morrow and HarperCollins are registered trademarks of HarperCollins Publishers in the United States of America and other countries.

FIRST EDITION

19 20 21 22 23 HDC 10 9 8 7 6 5 4 3 2 1

*This book is dedicated to everyone still searching
for their Happily Ever After.
Never stop believing.
Love often finds you when you least expect it . . .*

Chapter One

HALEY HANSON WAS right in the middle of one of those once-in-a-lifetime moments every girl supposedly dreams of. She was trying on a spectacular wedding dress. But looking at herself in the mirror, instead of feeling overjoyed, she almost felt—guilty, because this had never been her dream.

A successful career woman and the youngest partner at one of Boston's most prestigious advertising agencies, Haley had always been more of a realist than a fairy-tale kind of girl. But somehow, in the most unlikely way, she had found her HEA, her Happily Ever After.

Meeting Jeff had changed everything.

Even as she thought about him now, she had to catch her breath. He had a way of doing that to her, taking her breath away. His love, his kindness, his dedication to family, his passion for life and his work, and most of all, his unconditional love for her had opened a door to a future she had never dared dream of. The fact that he was also incredibly handsome was just a bonus.

From the moment she had met Jeff and his dad, Ben, at Christmas Camp a year ago, the path she had always been on shifted. With Jeff, her journey to find love had been far from easy. There were bumpy roads, wrong turns, detours, and delays, but in the end, she knew that right now, even if this hadn't been a dream she'd grown up with, she was exactly where she was meant to be, standing on a dressing room platform, inside one of Boston's beautiful boutique bridal stores.

As she did a slow spin in front of the mirror, taking in her stunning silk-sheath wedding dress, she still couldn't believe how trusting her heart had led her here.

It was really happening.

She was marrying Jeff in forty-eight hours, on Christmas Eve!

She still couldn't believe how fast the last year had flown by. The last few months especially were a blur, planning the wedding while helping Jeff's dad franchise his Christmas Camp concept.

When she first pitched Ben the idea, she believed it would be successful, but nothing had prepared them for the overwhelming response of people wanting to do the Christmas Camps, not just in the United States but in Europe, as well.

Working in advertising, she knew one of the keys to being successful was creating something people needed.

She had learned firsthand just how powerful and life changing a Christmas Camp experience could be. She knew the day she had given up a prestigious national account to help Ben launch the Christmas Camp franchise idea that she was doing the right thing, just like she knew now, two days before her wedding, that she was marrying the right person for all the right reasons.

The fact that she had no doubts left her with an incredible sense of gratitude and wonder at how this could now be her life. She had gone from being nicknamed the Grinch to having her own Christmas miracle.

As her sparkling oval-cut engagement ring caught the light, she smiled remembering how Jeff had proposed to her at the same place his dad had proposed to his mom, at Star Peak, overlooking a breathtaking snow-covered mountain range.

Jeff had started off by having them both look for a pinecone so they could make a Christmas wish together, a tradition in Jeff's family. After he had helped Haley pick the perfect pinecone, she had found a stunning engagement ring tucked inside. Jeff had told her it was his dad's idea to use diamonds from his mom's wedding ring to have a special ring created just for her, to continue the tradition of true love. He had then gotten down on one knee and proposed, saying how much he loved her and that he wanted to spend every Christmas together for the rest of their lives.

Knowing that Jeff had proposed to her at Star Peak, just like his dad had proposed to his mom, meant everything to her. Now that his mom had passed away, she knew it was even more important to him to honor her memory by keeping special traditions like this alive.

Haley would be the first to admit that when she first met Jeff and his dad, Christmas traditions weren't exactly her thing. That's why her boss, Larry, had sent her to Holly Peak Inn, to Christmas Camp, to find her Christmas spirit, hoping it would help her land a huge new holiday advertising campaign.

For years, Haley's idea of celebrating Christmas meant getting out of town and taking her parents to the Caribbean to avoid all the Christmas craziness and celebrating the holiday. While her parents would vacation on the beach, she would always work, using the time not celebrating Christmas to get ahead, while her competitors took time off.

But as soon as Haley had arrived at Christmas Camp, she quickly found there was no avoiding the Christmas craziness there. She was surrounded by Christmas 24–7, from the decorations, to the activities, to the meals, you name it. If it had anything to do with Christmas, it was happening at Christmas Camp. Haley had desperately wanted to escape, but when her boss insisted she stay the entire week, all she could do was try to find ways to avoid all the holiday hoopla. But every time she tried to take a shortcut, she kept running into one big roadblock.

Jeff.

Jeff's dad, Ben, owned the inn and ran the Christmas Camp, so Jeff had made it his personal mission to keep an eye on Haley. He'd known she didn't want to be there and had told her he wanted to make sure she didn't wreck the other guests' experiences. That's when she had nicknamed him the "Christmas Camp Police."

But what had started out as Christmas Camp chaos had turned into something much more meaningful for Haley. Through Christmas Camp, she was able to learn what mattered most at Christmas—family, friends, community, and love—and was then able to open her heart to finding her Christmas spirit and finding true love.

If someone had told her back then that the following Christmas she'd be marrying the "Christmas Camp Police," she would have laughed them all the way to the North Pole.

But yet, here she was, wearing a wedding dress. It was crazy. Christmas crazy, in a good way.

Haley twirled around one more time in front of the mirror. "So what do you think?" She looked over at her best friend, Kathy, who was enjoying the posh surroundings, lounging on a white velvet settee, sipping champagne.

Kathy lifted her glass in a toast. "I think it's perfect for you. It's simple but chic, classy but not stuffy, expensive but not showy. It's totally you. I love it!"

Haley smiled brightly. "So do I. They did a great job with the alterations."

"It's going to be perfect for the pictures," Kathy said.

"I hope so." Haley reverently touched her silky dress.

"You know, at first, I only agreed to do all of this—the designer dress, the fancy cake, and all the flowers—because my mom and dad needed some promotional pictures to get ready to open their B&B. But now, honestly, I'm really getting into it. I guess it's happened. I've officially caught bridal fever."

"And why not?" Kathy said. "You only do this once. You deserve this."

"I'm just glad I was able to get everyone to donate everything in exchange for all the publicity this will hopefully bring them."

Kathy nodded. "Your parents are lucky they have a brand specialist for a daughter who can work her magic and make all these things happen."

"I'm just thankful all the renovations are finally done at the Money Pit, in time for the wedding, and to open after Christmas," Haley said.

Kathy gave her a look. "Hey, remember, you're not supposed to call it the Money Pit anymore? That's bad karma. It's now your parents' beautifully restored Victorian that's going to be one of the hottest B&Bs in Massachusetts."

Haley laughed. "As long as I'm still paying the bills on it, I'm calling it the Money Pit."

"Fair enough," Kathy said and smiled back at her.

A pretty salesclerk walked over to Haley holding a fabulous bejeweled tiara and veil. "Are you ready to try this on?" she asked.

Haley nodded, excited.

As the salesclerk arranged the veil, Haley shut her eyes.

"Okay, you can open your eyes now," she said.

When Haley opened her eyes and looked at her reflection in the mirror, she let out a small gasp. As she fought back tears of happiness, she couldn't believe this was really her life. She was getting married to a man who was better than any dream she'd ever had. "I feel like . . ."

"Cinderella?" Kathy asked.

"No," Haley laughed, breaking the spell. "I could never do those glass slippers." She thought about it for a moment, then smiled. "I feel like Meghan Markel in my own fairy tale."

They all laughed.

When Haley struck the perfect princess pose, Kathy snapped a quick picture with her phone. "Well, no one deserves a fairy tale more than you and Meghan." Kathy lifted her glass of champagne for a toast. "To the fairy tale . . ."

Haley held out her empty hands. "Wait, where's my champagne?"

Kathy was already pouring her a glass. "After you get out of your dress."

"I think that's our cue," the salesclerk said to Haley, as she led her back into the dressing room and carefully help her out of her dress. Haley, with a grateful smile, handed her the veil and tiara. "Thank you, this is all perfect."

The salesclerk smiled back at her. "We'll have it all ready for you up front. You're going to look beautiful. This dress is perfect on you. We can't wait to see the pictures."

"Thank you, again, for everything." Haley gave her a grateful smile.

A few minutes later, Haley came out of the dressing room wearing chic black pants, strappy high heels, and a sapphire-blue leather coat. She looked every inch the success she was.

When Kathy handed her a glass of champagne, they clinked glasses. "Now we can toast together. To my best friend getting married, chasing her dreams, and creating her own happily ever after. You're my inspiration.

Haley gave Kathy a heartfelt hug. "And thank you for being here and doing all this with me."

Kathy sipped her champagne, smiled. "You're my best friend. Where else would I be? Plus, I love the dress I get to wear." Kathy walked over to a gorgeous burgundy velvet cocktail dress that was hanging up.

"Only the best for my best woman," Haley said. "It really is going to look amazing on you."

"I love that you're not calling me your maid of honor," Kathy said. "The word 'maid' is too close to the word 'old maid,' and I don't need to be reminded . . ."

Haley laughed. "We're only thirty-three. You're not an old maid."

"Yeah, well tell that to my dating app where all the guys only want to date hot twenty-year-olds."

"Then you need to find a better place to meet guys," Haley said.

"Well, one of those places is supposed to be a wedding, but then you decided to have this small, intimate wedding, so you're not helping me out one bit."

Haley laughed. "So, you're saying I should have done a big wedding so you could meet someone?"

Kathy poured herself more champagne. "Exactly. You're supposed to help me get my HEA."

Haley put her arm around her. "I'm sorry I let you down on this one, but I know your happily ever after is just around the corner. Jeff's dad always says at Christmas anything is possible. You just have to believe."

Kathy laughed. "And to think a year ago I was calling you Grinchy."

Haley grinned back at her. "I guess my heart has grown three sizes, just like the Grinch's."

"And then some," Kathy agreed.

Haley put down her champagne glass. "Now that we're done here, I need to head over to the Money Pit to make sure everything's perfect for our shoot. We need some great pictures to launch the B&B's website and social media pages."

Kathy gave her a look. "You mean you need to go to your parents' fabulous B&B?"

Haley laughed.

"You know, it really does look amazing now that the renovations are finally done. Jeff did a great job helping finish everything up."

Haley agreed. "The perks of marrying an architect who specializes in restoration projects. I think he loves our old Victorian as much as my parents do. They all see the potential . . ."

"Where you've only seen the problems," Kathy finished for her.

"Well, there have certainly been enough of them, but thankfully, that's all in the past," Haley said. "So, do you want to come with me? We're shooting the wedding cake and flower pictures today. I could use your creative eye. You are one of my favorite graphic designers at work."

Kathy arched an eyebrow. "One of your favorites?"

Haley laughed. "Sorry, I meant my favorite, first and foremost, and always and forever."

"Okay, now you just sound like you're practicing your wedding vows."

Haley's smile faded. "Thanks for reminding me. I still have to write them."

Kathy looked surprised. "You haven't written them yet? You're getting married in forty-eight hours."

Haley shook her head. "I know. I need to do it. I've just been so busy with everything, I haven't had a chance."

"I'm sure you'll come up with something fabulous. You come up with slogans and advertising copy for a living. Piece of cake."

Haley smiled, nodded. She didn't want to admit to Kathy, or anyone else, that she had tried to write her vows several times, but she could never seem to find the right words. She wanted everything to be perfect, starting with this first photo shoot. "Okay, let's get going." Haley headed for the checkout counter where the salesclerk was waiting with both of their dresses. "Are you with me?"

Kathy caught up with her. "Always."

"And wait until you see the incredible cake." Haley got out her phone and showed Kathy a picture of it. The cake was amazing! It was snow white, with six different tiers all in the shape of different squares. It looked like a bundle of Christmas presents all wrapped up with an elaborate burgundy fondant bow.

"Whoa! That's some cake." Kathy looked impressed. "I've never seen anything like that. It's supposed to be Christmas presents, right?"

"Right." Haley brought up another picture to show her. "I actually saw this picture of it after it won a pastry competition in Paris."

"Nice," Kathy said.

"Right? And you know Jean Michael on Newbury Street? He was able to re-create it for me. It took forever to make, but it was worth it. Look how beautiful it is."

Kathy gave Haley's hand a little squeeze. "This is going to be the perfect wedding."

Haley nodded. "And I'm getting really excited."

"Just don't turn into a Bridezilla on me," Kathy said.

Haley laughed. "Never." She was about to say something else when her phone rang. She was surprised to see it was Jeff calling on FaceTime. She picked up quickly.

"Hey babe, what's up? I thought you were going to be in meetings all day?"

Jeff's handsome face looked troubled. "I was, but . . ."

Haley looked at the phone closer. "Wait, are you at my parents' house?" Her eyes grew huge. "And what's happening behind you? Is that water pouring out of the ceiling?"

Jeff took a deep breath. "Haley, you need to get over here right away. We have to cancel the wedding."

Chapter Two

HALEY AND KATHY stood in her parents' living room and looked around in shock. The scene was horrific. Water was still dripping from the ceiling, and there were buckets of water everywhere. Plastic sheets covered all the furniture and the floors.

"I can't believe this . . ." Haley's voice was overcome with emotion. "Are my parents okay?"

Jeff came over and put his arm around her and cradled her close. "Your parents are fine. They went out to the tree farm to get some fresh garland and holly for the wedding. I've already called them. They're heading back now. So, no one was here to know a pipe had burst until I stopped by to drop off some things for the wedding."

Haley still couldn't believe what she was seeing. As she looked over to the massive dining room table, her shock turned into sadness. "Oh no . . ." She looked up at Jeff.

He looked just as sad. "I know. I'm sorry."

On the table was what used to be her exquisite designer wedding cake. It now didn't look like a cake at all. Instead it was just a lumpy puddle of flour and frosting. The deep crimson stream of melted fondant running across the table made it look like a wedding cake crime scene.

As Haley walked over for a closer look, her heart hurt. The cake had meant something special to her. She always said that Jeff's love was the best Christmas gift she had ever received and having her cake designed to look like Christmas presents symbolized that.

And the cake wasn't the only thing destroyed. All of Haley's flowers for the wedding, dozens and dozens of red and white roses, that she had been getting ready to use for the photo shoot, were now all soggy and drooping, with their petals falling off.

It made her sick to her stomach, realizing that her perfect plan to launch her parents' new B&B and to have a dream wedding had gone the way of the *Titanic*. Everything was underwater.

Haley looked up at the water still dripping from the ceiling. "So, what happened?"

"A pipe burst in the bathroom upstairs," Jeff said. "By the time I got here, most of the damage was done. I already have a plumber upstairs, and we'll be able to put down a new floor tomorrow, and we'll get this place cleaned up really fast."

Haley gave Jeff a hopeful look. "How fast? In time for our wedding on Christmas Eve?"

Jeff shook his head. "No, I'm sorry. Not that fast. We have to check out the electrical and make sure everything is safe. No one can stay here until we get the all clear."

When Haley laughed, it almost sounded like a cry. As she picked up one of the wet rose bouquets, water dripped off the petals. "Everything's ruined." She looked over to Kathy, who was standing silently in the corner. "You were right. I jinxed this place by still calling it the Money Pit, and I also jinxed my wedding. We're going to have to call the whole thing off."

"There has to be something we can do," Kathy said. Still, she cringed when she looked over at the dining room table.

"Right," Jeff said. He was quick to come to Haley's side and take her hand. "We're not calling off the wedding. We can order another cake and flowers. It'll be fine. The place doesn't matter. As long as we have our friends and each other."

Haley, still reeling from the shock, gave him an incredulous look. "We can't just find another place. It's two days to Christmas. Everything's booked. Nothing's available. That's one of the reasons we decided to have it here in the first place. And your friend Steve, the best man, he's flying in from LA. He was supposed to stay here and so was your dad and everyone else, so we could all spend Christmas together after the wedding." Haley's voice was getting higher and higher. She knew she was starting to spiral out of control, but she couldn't help herself. All she could think about was how disappointed her parents were going to be. She had come up with the perfect plan to have her wedding at the B&B to get the publicity photos for the website and now none of that was going to happen. "This is a nightmare."

Jeff grabbed both of her hands and looked into her eyes. "It's going to be okay."

"How?" Haley asked. She was close to tears. "My parents planned to open right after Christmas. They have worked so hard on this. This is their dream."

"And they'll still be able to open on time. It looks a lot worse than it is," Jeff said. "I promise you. I already have guys lined up who said they'll work around the clock getting this place fixed up."

"But if we can't have the wedding here, we can't do all the publicity photos for them."

"You have all those other photos that are great," Jeff said. "You have more than enough for the website."

"But they don't show a wedding, and everyone loves a wedding. That's why we were doing this."

"I thought we were doing this because we love each other and wanted to get married," Jeff said in a teasing voice. Haley knew he was just trying to lighten the moment, but right now she felt like the weight of the world was on her shoulders.

Kathy came over. She had a more positive look on her face now. "Jeff's right. The other photos we've already shot are fantastic. Your parents are going to be fine. Right now, we just need to concentrate on where you're going to get married. That's the most important thing."

Haley didn't look like she agreed.

Jeff looked into Haley's eyes. "Kathy's right. I love you. I want to marry you, and I don't care where or how we do it."

"I want to marry you, too, but it's not that easy," Haley said. "It's almost Christmas. Most places are either booked or closed."

Jeff put his arm around her. "I've already made a call, and I've worked everything out."

Haley and Kathy both gave him a skeptical look.

"You found us a place to get married and for everyone to stay?" Haley asked.

Jeff kissed the top of her head. "I did, and it's perfect."

"Where?" Kathy asked. "Because Haley's right. Everything's booked."

When Jeff smiled at them both, he looked quite pleased with himself. "Except us. We never book the inn at Christmas. That time is just for family."

Haley's eyes grew huge. "You want us to get married at Christmas Camp?!"

Jeff nodded as he looked into her eyes. "It's where we met, fell in love, where I proposed—it's perfect."

Haley shook her head, trying to take it all in. Jeff's

dad's Holly Peak Inn was in a remote area, up in the woods. It had a special rustic charm, but Haley couldn't even imagine how they could ever pull off a wedding there. "But I thought your dad shuts down now until New Year's," Haley said just as some more water from the ceiling dripped on her head. Jeff quickly pulled her out of the way.

"He is shut down, so he could be here for the wedding, but I've already called him, and he's called Laura, and she's going to help, as well, and they're going to open back up just for us," Jeff said.

"Who's Laura?" Kathy asked.

"She's the chef I told you about that did the Christmas Camp," Haley answered.

Kathy smiled and nodded. "The one who made the Christmas cookies you loved."

"That's the one," Jeff said. "We all love those cookies, and now she can make them for the wedding. I'm sure she can make a wedding cake, as well."

Haley gave Jeff an incredulous look. "It's not that easy to just whip up a wedding cake, especially when she'll have to do all the other meals, as well. We can't ask her to do all that."

"Laura volunteered," Jeff said, "and you know how she's practically part of the family. She was coming to the wedding anyway."

Haley looked stressed. "Coming to the wedding and working the wedding are two different things."

Jeff wasn't fazed by her tone. "The point is, everyone

can help. They're all waiting for us to get up there. We can make this work. Think of it as an adventure."

Haley stared at Jeff. She didn't look happy. "So now our wedding's an adventure? We've gone from our goal of having it be picture-perfect to get publicity shots for my parents' B&B to an adventure. Seriously? What else can go wrong?"

"Don't say that!" Kathy grabbed Haley's hand. "You'll jinx us again." Kathy looked so serious it made Haley laugh and for that she was grateful.

She knew she needed to stop having a pity party and put things in perspective. While the burst pipe had caused a huge mess and meant canceling the wedding at her parents', no one was hurt, and that was the most important thing. Everything in the house could be fixed, everything but her beautiful wedding cake. Just as Haley looked over at the cake again, more drops of water from the ceiling dripped into the puddle of what used to be her cake, making the already gooey mess even more pathetic looking.

As she looked over at Jeff, there was only one thing she knew for sure, how much she loved him, and he was right. It didn't matter where or how they got married as long as they got married and started their lives together as a team. That was the important thing.

If she was honest with herself, it was when she had decided to combine her wedding with her personal work project to help get publicity for her parents' B&B that she had gotten swept up into the whole perfect wedding thing. She knew right now she was dangerously close to being one of those Bridezillas you always hear about instead of just being thankful she had a great guy in the first place who loved her and wanted to spend the rest of his life with her.

She mentally pulled herself together and walked over to Jeff and gave him a kiss.

He looked surprised in a good way. "What was that for?"

"For being you. I love you, and you're right, the rest doesn't matter. We can even go down to City Hall and get married. I don't care."

"Actually, you can't," Kathy said. "It's closed for the holidays."

Haley laughed. "Okay, no City Hall."

"We don't need City Hall, we have Christmas Camp," Jeff said. He looked excited. "You'll see—it's going to be great. We already have all the beautiful decorations set up at the inn for Christmas Camp, and the rooms are ready. This can totally work. Dad even has a wedding planner already pulling things together for us."

Haley looked surprised. "How in the world did your dad find a wedding planner at the last minute like this?"

Jeff shrugged. "You know my dad. He said something about knowing someone who knew someone or something, but the point is, we can make this work. Right?"

When Haley looked into his eyes, she remembered all the reasons she loved him so much, including his always-positive can-do attitude. She took a deep breath and smiled. "We can make it work. Let the adventure begin."

Jeff, looking relieved, pulled her into his arms for a heartfelt hug. "That's the spirit."

Haley laughed. "The Christmas spirit? Is this another Christmas Camp lesson?"

"Hey, you said it. Not me," Jeff laughed. "But you know what my dad would say."

Haley looked into Jeff's eyes. "He would love it."

"Just like I love you."

When they kissed, Kathy waited a few seconds then cleared her throat. "Okay, you two lovebirds. Stop it. We have a wedding to plan."

Jeff laughed. "She's right. You just need to go home and pack and get up to the inn as fast as you can. Dad says the wedding planner is waiting to meet you. I'll go to the airport and pick up Steve. We'll share a room to make space for everyone else. It'll be just like at college. It'll all work out. Don't worry. I'll see you at the inn. I already told your parents the plan. They're heading up as soon as they get back and grab some stuff. I'll also let Gail know what's happening."

"Gail's not already up there with your dad?" Haley asked. "I thought she was helping him with the Christmas Camps?"

"She has been, but she came back into Boston yesterday, thinking the wedding was here," Jeff said. "She said something about wanting to get her hair and nails done, all that girl stuff. So, now I told her the change of plans, and she's getting what she needs and heading back tomorrow morning."

Haley turned to Kathy. "Gail was part of my Christmas Camp group, and she and Ben hit it off."

"What about the rest of the Christmas Camp crew that was coming?" Haley asked.

"I already texted John, and he's letting everyone know."

"Are these the guys who did the camp with you last year?" Kathy asked.

Haley nodded. "They're all great. I can't wait for you to meet them. There's John and his two kids, Madison and Blake, and then Ian and Susie, this fun couple in their twenties. Susie is Miss Christmas. You'll love her."

"They all sound great," Kathy said. "I can't wait."

"My boss, Larry, is traveling for the holidays to see his daughters, and so are a lot of other friends. We knew that was going to happen, but it was really important for us to get married during Christmas."

"So, we're just doing a really small wedding now, and then, we'll have a big party in January to celebrate with everyone," Jeff said. "But when the Christmas Camp crew heard about the wedding, they all wanted to come."

Haley looked worried. "That's when it was in the city. You're sure everyone's okay with heading up to the mountains to the inn?"

Jeff laughed. "Are you kidding? John said he's really excited to get out of the city, and the kids have been talking about all the fun things they did at Christmas Camp last year and they want to go sledding again, so they're thrilled."

Kathy looked so excited. "I am loving this Christmas Camp already."

Jeff gave Kathy a high five. "Just wait until you get there. Okay, so the new plan is, everyone's coming up tomorrow morning, the day before the wedding, and we'll have the wedding on Christmas Eve, as planned."

Haley looked impressed. "Wow, okay. So this could really work."

"Of course it will work. It's going to be great," Jeff said. "But you should get going. You know how the roads can be this time of year. You want to get up there tonight before dark. I have to go get Steve, and we'll meet you girls up there." Jeff kissed Haley one more time before heading out. "Love you."

"Love you, too."

As soon as Jeff left, Haley stood there, looking at the dripping ceiling. She looked a little dazed.

"You okay?" Kathy asked.

Haley nodded. "I guess. I just can't believe how quickly all our wedding plans have changed."

Kathy walked over to the dining room table. She picked up a soggy rose. "Is there anything we can salvage here and take up with us?"

When Haley looked at the sad little rose, she shook her head. "No. Let's just get going. I still have to take back my wedding dress. They were only letting me have it as a trade for the publicity they would be getting, but now that there's not going to be any photos or publicity . . ."

"No dress?" Kathy asked. She looked bummed.

"Exactly," Haley said with a sigh.

"What are you going to wear?"

Haley shrugged. "It doesn't really matter. Now it's just going to be a small casual wedding up in the woods. I'm sure I have something that will work."

Kathy came over and linked arms with Haley. "It's gonna be okay. You'll see. You're always saying, anything's possible at Christmas. You just have to believe."

Haley took a deep breath as they headed for the front door. "I believe Jeff is right. This is going to be one big adventure."

Chapter Three

DRIVING THE LAST stretch of winding mountain road to the Holly Peak Inn, Haley was thankful that the roads had recently been plowed and were clear of snow and ice. All around her, it looked like a winter wonderland. A blanket of fresh snow covered the hillside and clung to the tree branches.

She thought about the first time she'd come up to Christmas Camp, when her boss had made her come. At that time, she hadn't even noticed the spectacular scenery. All she had cared about was getting up to the inn and getting the whole Christmas Camp experience done as soon as possible so she could get back to work in Boston. It seemed like a lifetime ago, not just a year ago.

"It really is so beautiful up here," Kathy said. She was taking pictures with her phone.

"And we couldn't have gotten a better day for a drive," Haley said.

The sky was clear and a brilliant sapphire blue, and the sun was just starting to set, making all the snow shimmer and sparkle.

Kathy nodded and kept taking pictures. "This really does look like a Christmas dream. I feel like we're living in one of those Christmas movies."

Haley laughed. "Right? And who doesn't want to do that. I feel like I have to pinch myself every time I come up here to make sure it's real. But Jeff and I have been so busy at work—he has been restoring another wharf on the waterfront, and I've been working nonstop on Ben's Christmas Camp franchise, plus helping my parents get ready to launch their B&B—we haven't been up since Thanksgiving."

"Do you usually come up more?" Kathy asked.

"Jeff likes to come up as much as possible to help his dad with the Christmas Camps, but now that Gail's been helping so much, it's worked out well for all of us."

"So Jeff's okay with that?" Kathy asked. "Gail and his dad?"

"Oh absolutely. We love Gail. She's amazing," Haley said. "I know Jeff's really happy his dad has someone to spend time with so he's not up here all alone. Plus, Gail loves helping out with the Christmas Camps. It's really a perfect fit. They're so cute together. You'll see."

"I can't believe how fast the Christmas Camp franchise has taken off," Kathy said. "You've been working nonstop since you got the idea."

Haley smiled. "I know, but it's worth it. I love thinking about how many people can experience the Christmas Camps now, and the numbers just keep going up. Did I tell you my parents are considering doing a Christmas Camp at the B&B?"

"What? No. That's so cool," Kathy said. "The B&B would be perfect for people who can't get away up here to the mountains but still want the experience."

"That's the idea, but first we have to the get the place open." Haley already had ideas for her parents' B&B having the Christmas Camps. She could even see the pictures on the website. She knew it would just mean more work for her, but she didn't mind. She loved her job and she loved doing everything she could to help Jeff's dad share the Christmas Camp experience. Jeff kept telling her she needed to hire an assistant, but at this point, she felt she needed to be completely hands-on to get the franchise off the ground properly.

She knew Ben had put his life savings into launching the franchise, and she wasn't going to let him or Jeff down. She'd also had a lot invested personally and professionally. This franchise idea was her baby, and she was going to make sure it grew up just the way it should. She didn't want it to grow too fast and lose the authenticity of what made the Christmas Camps so special.

"We're almost here," Haley said as she took the last

turn to the Holly Peak Inn. As they drove slowly down the meandering tree-lined road, Kathy took more pictures.

"Wow, it's even more amazing than the website pictures. You need to update their website," Kathy said.

Haley laughed. "Thanks, another job. Just what I need." She smiled at Kathy. "No, seriously, you're right. Get me some good pictures, and I'll put them up."

"Deal," Kathy said.

As they turned the last corner and the Holly Peak Inn came into full view, Kathy was so in awe she forgot to take pictures.

"Wow!" Kathy said, taking it all in. "I can't believe all the Christmas decorations."

Haley laughed. "Oh, you haven't seen anything yet. Just wait. I told you. Jeff's dad, Ben, goes all out for Christmas and his Christmas Camps."

Haley parked the car. "Looks like we beat Jeff here."

When they both got out of the car, Kathy looked around in awe.

"I love it here," Kathy said, linking arms with Haley.

"Me, too," Haley said as they both stood and admired the quaint and charming inn. It was tucked away in the woods and outlined with white twinkling Christmas lights. All the surrounding trees were also glowing. They were covered with red, green, silver, and gold Christmas lights. The inn was a pristine white with black shutters, and on every window there was a beautiful wreath made out of fresh fir tree branches, holly, and pinecones. The largest wreath was on the front door.

The whole setting was dreamlike.

Before Haley could even get their bags out of the trunk, she was greeted with a loud bark, as Max, Ben's adorable golden retriever, came racing toward them.

"Max!" Haley got down onto one knee, so she could give him a hug. He was the first friend she'd made at Christmas Camp, and she loved him dearly.

Max looked just as excited to see her. He was wagging his tail and licking her face.

Kathy laughed. "Does Jeff know about this relationship? Because clearly this is your first love."

"Oh, he knows," Haley said. "Doesn't he, Max. He knows you're my favorite."

"Hey, I heard that!" Ben said. He was laughing and looked excited to see them.

"Ben!" Haley rushed over to him and gave him a heartfelt hug. "I've missed you!"

He smiled, as he hugged her back. "We talk almost every day."

"Email and calls aren't the same, and that's all about work . . ."

Ben nodded and looked into her eyes. "And for the next few days, no work. You know my rules at Christmas Camp. To be in the moment and enjoy what's around you, and of course, get you married to my son!"

They all shared a laugh.

"Ben, this is my best friend, and coworker, Kathy. She's actually worked on the Christmas Camp franchise. She's the best graphic designer in Boston."

Kathy came over and took Ben's hand. "And now you see why we're friends. It's so wonderful to finally meet you. I've heard so much about you from both Haley and Jeff."

Ben took her hand and pulled Kathy in for a hug. "And I've heard so much about you. Welcome."

Max barked.

Haley laughed. "Max welcomes you, too."

Kathy leaned down to pet him, and Max loved every minute of it.

Haley looked around at all the decorations. "The place looks great. It looks like you put up some new things."

Ben's eyes twinkled. "You have to keep things fresh. Isn't that what you say?"

Haley laughed and put her arm around Ben. "Actually, it is. If I'm not careful you're going to be taking my job." They both laughed, as Haley continued to look around. "And I see you have Jeff's favorite reindeer ready to go." Haley motioned over to a group of life-sized LED wired reindeer set up like they were about to pull Santa's sleigh.

"Of course," Ben said. "It wouldn't be Christmas without the reindeer."

Kathy walked over so she could get a closer look. "These are great. What's the story with the reindeer? You said they're Jeff's favorite?"

Ben and Haley shared a knowing smile.

"Ben's mom got them when he was little," Ben said.

"He was so excited when he saw them all set up, waiting for Santa, until he couldn't find one with a red nose."

"And he was convinced Rudolph had gotten lost," Haley said.

"Oh no, poor, Jeff," Kathy said.

"But his mom came to the rescue," Ben said. "That night when Jeff was sleeping, she made a red nose and put it on one of the reindeer. She then moved it so it was a little bit away from the rest of the group, like it maybe had gotten lost, and when she took Jeff out the next morning, and he saw it, he was over the moon happy. He was convinced that Rudolph had used his nose to find his way home."

"Of course," Haley said.

Kathy laughed. "That's too cute."

"The kids still love it, and so do we," Ben said. "We have a lot of wonderful memories here. Every year, we try to make more, and now look at the one we'll be making this year!"

"I can't wait to be part of it," Kathy said.

Haley took Ben's hand and looked into his eyes. "Thank you so much for doing all of this last minute for the wedding. Don't worry—we're not planning anything fancy. We can just do a little ceremony on Christmas Eve. My dad is the officiate. He got his license, figuring it could come in handy at the B&B, so we'll just keep things really simple."

Ben chuckled. "I'm thrilled that you're here and that we can have the wedding here. I know Jeff's mom would be so pleased," Ben said. "We haven't had a wedding here before, and I can't think of a better wedding to start with. And don't worry, we have a wedding planner, so she can help with everything. You can just relax and enjoy this moment. So let's get inside, so you can meet her. We don't have any time to waste."

Kathy turned to Haley and gave her a confident smile. "See, this is all going to work out great."

Haley nodded, as they followed Ben and Max to the inn.

"It is," Ben agreed. He sounded upbeat and chipper. "You don't worry about a thing. You're here now. We've got everything under control. Laura's already putting together some menu options for you, and Gail's coming back up tomorrow, and she can't wait to help out, too. We're all very excited about this."

Haley gave Ben a knowing look. "So, how's everything going with you and Gail? She's been spending a lot of time up here."

Ben smiled like a man in love and blushed a little. It was endearing. "I'm one lucky guy for sure," he said. "Gail's wonderful. She loves helping out with the Christmas Camps, and the guests love her, too. She has some really great ideas that we've added and some new decorating ideas. I can't wait to show you."

"And?" Haley waited. She gave Ben a teasing look. She wasn't about to let him off the hook. She wanted to hear him say it.

Ben laughed. "And she has been great company. Gail is a very special person."

"Yes, she is," Haley agreed. She loved seeing Ben look so happy. "And she says the same about you."

Kathy looked intrigued. "So, wait, Haley, you met Jeff here at Christmas Camp, and Ben, you met Gail. This sounds more like a Matchmaker Christmas Camp to me, and if that's the case, sign me up. I'm still waiting to meet my Prince Charming."

Ben and Haley laughed.

When they got to the front door, Haley smiled at the adorable life-sized elf figurine. "Looking good, little guy," she said as she patted his head.

Kathy cheerfully patted the elf's head, too. "Does this bring you good luck?"

Haley laughed. "I don't know about that."

"Well you met Jeff here so I'm going to do whatever you do," Kathy said. She looked completely serious.

When Ben opened the door for them Haley's face lit up. Laura was waiting with an adorable reindeer tray that was holding colorful Santa mugs that all had huge swirls of whipped cream on top and candy canes for stir sticks.

"Laura! It's so good to see you," Haley said.

"Merry Christmas," Laura said. Her smile was genuine and warm. "I thought you might want some Christmas Camp hot chocolate to help warm you up."

Haley laughed as she took a Santa mug. "Laura, you

know me so well. Thank you." Haley handed the mug to Kathy. "You're going to love this."

Kathy gave Laura an excited look. "Oh, I've heard all about this hot chocolate." She took a quick sip and blissfully shut her eyes. "Yup, it's just as good as Haley promised. Amazing. Thank you."

Haley took the other mug and gave Laura a heartfelt smile. "I'm so glad you're here and not just because of this hot chocolate."

"You know I wouldn't have missed this for the world," Laura said.

Haley looked grateful. "And you've probably already guessed but this is my best friend, Kathy."

Laura smiled at Kathy. "It's so good to finally meet you. I've heard so much about you.

"Not as much as I've heard about you," Kathy smiled back at her. "And if I'm not mistaken you're also responsible for the famous cookies Haley hasn't stopped talking about."

Everyone laughed.

"That would be me," Laura said. "And I have a batch in the oven right now."

Haley gave Kathy a look. "Watch out. They're addicting."

Haley took Laura's hand. "Thank you for doing all this for me. Are you sure it's okay? I don't want to take you away from your family at Christmas."

Laura laughed. "Are you kidding? My husband is thrilled to get to watch football all day, and we're seeing our kids next week when we go to my daughter's house in Florida, so this worked out great."

"If you're sure . . ." Haley said.

Laura took Haley's hand and gave it a little squeeze. "I'm sure that nothing would make me happier than being a part of your special day. When are your parents coming up?"

"Tomorrow morning, so they can get everything settled at the B&B."

Ben smiled at Haley. "I talked to them and promised them you were in good hands and that we had everything under control here."

Haley looked touched. "Thank you so much for coming to the rescue. I can't tell you what this all means to me."

Ben put his arm around her. "We're family. This is what family does, and we all love you very much. We can't wait to officially make you part of the family."

When Max barked and wagged his tail, everyone laughed.

"We're all looking forward to it," Ben said. "Especially Max."

As they all followed Ben into the sitting room, Haley smiled when she saw all the stockings hanging from the fireplace. There was one with her name on it that also had a pretty angel on it. It was the same stocking Ben had first given her when she had arrived at Christmas Camp a year ago.

Kathy looked mesmerized by the room full of Christmas decorations. She turned around slowly, taking everything in, from Ben's impressive Santa figurine collection, to a variety of beautiful snow globes, to all the colorful nutcrackers lined up by the fireplace. "This really is like a Christmas dream." Her look of wonder grew when she spotted the giant Christmas tree in the corner. She walked over and looked at all the unique handmade ornaments. "And this tree. I don't think I've ever seen one like it."

Ben joined her at the tree. "No, you haven't. This is our special Christmas Camp tree. Every guest who comes to the camp has to make an ornament to hang on the tree using things that inspire them from nature or things they find around the inn. This was Haley's."

Haley laughed and covered her face, embarrassed, when Ben held up the dog biscuit ornament she had made. "I can't believe you kept it, or that Max didn't eat it."

"Oh, he sure tried," Ben said. "But I wouldn't let him. Your ornament and all the rest here are part of our Christmas Camp tradition. It's one of my favorite things, decorating with these ornaments every year and remembering everyone who made them. We all have to make one this year, too. After the wedding, when we have more time."

"I love that," Kathy said.

Haley smiled at Ben. "Me, too."

Laura picked up the tray Ben had put down. "Excuse me, everyone, but I need to get back in the kitchen and check on those cookies. Haley, as soon as you finalize the menu with Trisha for the wedding reception and dinner, just let us know and I'll start getting everything ready."

"Trisha?" Haley asked.

Ben's eyes lit up. "Your wedding planner. You're going to love her. She's in her room right now making a few calls, wedding planning stuff I think, but she'll be down soon. And don't worry, we saved the angel room for you."

Haley laughed. "Of course you did."

"And if it's okay, I'd love to go up to my room and get settled," Kathy said.

Ben grabbed Kathy's bags. "I'll be happy to show you your room. I put you in the star room—it's Gail's favorite."

Kathy looked excited. "That sounds great. Thank you."

As Ben led Kathy up the stairs, he turned back around and smiled at Haley. "Welcome home, Haley."

Haley gave him a grateful look. "Thank you. Thank you for everything."

After everyone was gone, Haley walked over to the fireplace where Max was curled up. He was watching her. "So, it looks like it's just you and me, Max."

"And me, if that's okay."

Haley looked up to see a very pretty girl walk into the room. She was in her early thirties, designer chic and perfectly put together from head to toe. She had a confidence about her that was impressive. She looked very much in control and at home at the inn.

"I'm Trisha, your wedding planner." Trisha held out her hand. "And you must be Haley, Jeff's girlfriend . . ."

Haley smiled, as she took her hand. "And now fiancée, bride-to-be. That's me."

Trisha was all business. She was already swiping through some pages on the computer tablet she was holding. "We should really get started. We don't have a lot of time."

Haley looked a little surprised by Trisha's intensity. "I don't know what Ben told you, and I'm so appreciative that you're here, but we're just going to do a really small, simple ceremony. We don't have time to do anything else."

When Trisha looked up from her tablet, she looked determined. "No matter how little time you have, we can still plan a proper wedding," Trisha said. "Don't you worry. This is what I do for a living, and I'm very good at it. That's why Ben asked for my help. I've already put some ideas together for you. Let's get started."

Without waiting for Haley's answer, Trisha headed for the couch. Haley quickly followed and sat down next to her. When Max came running over, Haley waited to pet him, but when he instead sat down at Trisha's feet, Haley looked surprised. "It looks like you've already made a friend with Max."

Trisha laughed as she leaned down to pet Max. "Oh, Max and I go way back. Don't we, boy?" When he happily tried to lick her face, she pulled back and gave him a stern look. "Max, you know the rule. No licking the face."

Haley looked confused. "So, you've been here before?"

Trisha smiled her perfect smile. "Yes, many times."

"But I didn't think they'd ever done a wedding here before?"

Trisha continued to pet Max. "Oh, they haven't. This will be a first. That's for sure."

Haley was feeling more confused by the second.

Trisha held up her tablet. "Here, let me show you my first idea."

Before Haley could ask any more questions, the front door opened, and Max took off running toward it. When Haley saw Jeff, she jumped up excitedly and went to the door.

"You made it," she said. "I was starting to worry."

Jeff kissed her quickly just as Steve came inside.

"Sorry, that was my fault," Steve said. "My plane was late."

Haley smiled at Steve. She had seen pictures of Jeff's college best friend, but they didn't do him justice. He was handsome, the same age as Jeff, in his midthirties, with a smile that could melt any girl's heart. Haley instantly liked him. "It's so good to finally meet you. I've heard so many stories."

Steve laughed. He pretended to look nervous. He patted Jeff on the back. "Don't believe anything this guy tells you, unless it's all good, then believe it all."

They all three laughed.

Steve stood back and smiled at Haley. "And you must be the beautiful bride, Haley." Steve gave her a hug. "You're obviously too good for this guy," he said, teasing. "Are you sure you don't want to rethink this whole wedding thing..."

Jeff playfully pushed Steve away from Haley. "Watch it, Romeo, she's all mine." When Jeff kissed Haley, she was still laughing.

She grabbed Jeff's hand. "Come in. You're just in time to meet our wedding planner."

"Great." As Jeff and Steve entered the sitting room with Haley, Trisha slowly stood up. She was smiling.

Steve looked surprised. "Trisha?"

Trisha came over and gave Steve a kiss on the cheek. "Steve, Merry Christmas."

Haley looked from Trisha to Steve. "You two know each other?"

When Steve whipped around to face Jeff, it was the first time she saw the look on Jeff's face. He looked surprised, and there was something else Haley couldn't quite define.

"What is it?" she asked Jeff.

But before Jeff could answer, Trisha walked up to him and gave him a kiss on the cheek, too, only this kiss lingered a little longer.

Trisha looked into Jeff's eyes. "Merry Christmas, Jeff."

Jeff finally found his voice. "Trisha, what are you doing here?"

Trisha smiled. "I'm your wedding planner."

Steve coughed, but it sounded more like he was choking.

Now Haley was totally confused. She looked at all three of them. "How do you all know each other?"

Jeff opened his mouth to say something, but before he could, Trisha jumped in.

"I met Steve through Jeff."

Haley looked at Trisha. She was still smiling at Jeff. But it wasn't just any ordinary smile, it was a flirty smile. Haley didn't know what was going on, except that she didn't like it. She turned to Jeff. "And how do you know Trisha?"

"I've been coming up here for years," Trisha answered for Jeff, never taking her eyes off him.

"As a guest?" Haley asked.

"No." Trisha laughed, as she continued looking at Jeff. "As his girlfriend."

Chapter Four

HALEY GAVE JEFF an incredulous look and waited for him to say something. When she noted how uncomfortable he looked, that made her even more concerned. When she looked over at Trisha, Trisha was smiling like she was as happy as could be. Haley, not liking how this was looking, turned back to Jeff.

"What's going on?" Haley asked.

Kathy interrupted the awkward moment by entering the room. "Hey, no fair having a party without me." She came over and hooked arms with Haley. "Introduce me to everyone."

Trisha held out her hand to Kathy. "Hi, I'm Trisha. I'm . . ."

"Jeff's girlfriend." Haley finished for her.

Kathy looked shocked. "Wait . . . What?"

Jeff jumped in. "My ex-girlfriend. She's my old girl-friend."

"And longtime friend of the family," Trisha said and smiled sweetly, too sweetly for Haley's liking.

Haley put her hands on her hips. She locked eyes with Jeff. "So, which is it? Old girlfriend or old family friend?"

Trisha walked over and stood next to Jeff and looked up at him. "It's both," she said. She was still smiling. Haley was not.

Haley turned to Kathy, who looked equally confused. "And she's my wedding planner."

Kathy's mouth dropped open. She quickly recovered, but you could still see the shock in her eyes.

Steve looked as uncomfortable as everyone else. "So, I was going to head into the kitchen. I think I smell Laura's cookies . . ."

Kathy immediately took the hint. "I'll go with you. I'm dying to try these cookies."

Steve looked over at Trisha. Trisha wasn't taking the hint. "Trisha, why don't you come with us? We can catch up. It's been a while."

As everyone stared at Trisha, it was clear she didn't want to leave.

Steve came over and put his arm around her. "Let's get caught up." As Steve started guiding Trisha away, she looked back at Jeff and smiled.

"But we need to catch up, too, Jeff," Trisha said. She

then looked at Haley. "I can't wait to hear all about how you met. It was a big surprise hearing about the wedding."

Steve walked faster. "Okay, let's go. Those cookies are waiting."

As soon as they were alone in the room, Haley turned to Jeff. She just looked at him. She didn't even know where to start. She had never heard about Trisha before.

"I can explain," Jeff said.

"Okay," Haley said. She walked over to the Christmas tree and pretended to study some ornaments when actually her mind was whirling a million miles a minute. She had questions, lots of questions. She turned back around and faced Jeff. "But first, just answer one thing. Is our wedding planner really your ex-girlfriend, because that just seems a little crazy . . ." When Haley saw Jeff take a deep breath, her eyes widened. "Okay. So it's true."

Jeff joined her over at the tree. He took her hand and looked into her eyes. "I swear I didn't know anything about this."

Haley let go of his hand and picked up a snow globe off the mantel and started shaking it, hard. "How long ago did you date? She clearly still has a thing for you."

Jeff, looking apologetic, gently took the snow globe out of her hand. He took a deep breath. "I've known Trisha a long time. I'm sure my dad was just trying to help and find someone fast. He's always treated her like family."

Haley stared at him. Hearing that Ben thought of Trisha as family only made Haley feel worse. "So when did you date? In college? Is that where you met?"

Jeff looked over at Max lying by the fireplace. Max put his head down on his paws. Jeff looked back at Haley. "No, we didn't meet in college."

Haley gave him an impatient look.

"We met here at the inn," Jeff said. He hesitated a moment. "When her family came for Christmas Camp."

Haley's eyes grew huge. She laughed, but it wasn't a happy laugh. "So, you met her at Christmas Camp, just like you met me? Okay, wow." Haley shook her head, trying to take it all in. "How long did you date?"

"Five years."

Haley's jaw dropped open. She didn't even try to pretend she was cool with that. "Five years. That's a long time, and you've never once mentioned her . . ."

"We haven't talked that much about exes."

Haley laughed. "That's because I didn't really have any serious old boyfriends. You know I've been concentrating on my career, but you apparently have had this serious relationship that I've known nothing about . . ."

"I didn't bring it up because Trisha's my past, and I want to concentrate on my future with you," Jeff said.

Haley started pacing around the room. "But yet here she is, your past, and she's about to become part of our future." Haley picked up a Santa figurine, stared at it, but didn't really see it.

"When did you break up?" Haley asked.

"About three years ago." Jeff answered.

Haley shook her head. "What I don't understand is, why would your dad ask your old girlfriend to be our wedding planner?"

"Because he has always liked Trisha," Jeff said. "When we were dating, we'd come up here all the time, and it wasn't a bad breakup. We parted as friends."

This made Haley feel even worse. "Then why did you break up?"

Jeff stared into the fire. "I broke things off after my mom passed away. I wanted to spend more time with my dad. He needed to be my number one focus. I didn't have time for a girlfriend."

Haley's heart was beating so fast, she had to take a breath. She was waiting for him to say they'd broken up because they weren't a good fit, because he didn't love her, not because his mom had passed away and he needed to take care of his dad.

Not wanting Jeff to see how upset and worried she was, she walked over to the window and looked out. As she watched the snow start to fall, she fought to stay calm. She couldn't help wondering now if Jeff had ever really gotten over Trisha. Five years was a long time to be with anyone. She'd only known Jeff a year and still couldn't believe how much she loved him. For the first time, she felt insecure about Jeff's love for her, and it was the worst feeling in the world. She felt sick to her stomach. Her mind was whirling. Doubt clawed at her heart.

What if Jeff had only broken up with Trisha because he was heartbroken about his mom, and now, now that he was better, now that he'd had some time to heal, his old feelings for Trisha could resurface. She took several deep breaths and willed herself to try to be rational and not jump to any conclusions, but she was scared, really scared. The thought of losing Jeff was unbearable.

When Jeff joined her at the window and put his arm around her, she didn't resist. Instead, she put her head on his shoulder; seeking the comfort he always gave her. He always made her feel loved. Not just by saying the words—and he did that a lot—but by the actions he did every day, the little things that showed her how much he cared. She had seen the way Trisha looked at him. It was clear she still had feelings for him, and now, Haley worried that Jeff, after seeing Trisha again, would also start to have feelings for her again, now that he had healed emotionally and was able to move on with his life.

"Haley, talk to me. What is it? Ask me anything, and you know I'll answer you."

Haley turned around. "Do you still have feelings for her?"

Jeff looked surprised. "What? For Trisha? No, of course not. You know I love you. We're getting married in two days."

"But you two only broke up because of what happened with your mom."

Jeff took Haley's hand and led her over to the couch

and sat down. "Honestly, I don't even remember everything that happened back then except how upset I was about losing my mom."

Haley looked worried. "That's what I mean. If that's the only reason you two broke up . . ."

Jeff looked into her eyes. "Here's what I do know. I love you. She's my past. You're my future. I know what I want, and I want to marry you on Christmas Eve . . ."

"With your old girlfriend being our wedding planner?" Haley said. She couldn't believe the words even as she said them.

When Jeff laughed a little, it only made Haley more upset.

"You better not be laughing at me. This isn't funny," she insisted.

Jeff took both her hands and pulled her toward him. He smiled as he looked into her eyes. "You're cute when you're jealous. I've never seen you jealous before."

Haley looked up at him. She didn't even try to deny it. "Because I've never had a reason to be before."

"And you don't have a reason now. I promise," Jeff said. "I'm not sure how all this went down. I'll talk to my dad, but I'm sure Trisha is just trying to help my dad and us and she's really good at what she does."

This didn't make Haley feel any better. She saw the way Trisha had looked at Jeff and even if Jeff was clueless, she knew Trisha still had feelings for him. Her spiraling thoughts were interrupted when Jeff gently lifted her chin so she was looking into his eyes.

"You're the only one I love," Jeff said. "You're stuck with me, this Christmas and every Christmas for the rest of our lives."

When he kissed her, Haley forgot about everything but the love she felt in that kiss. It was the perfect kiss— until they were interrupted.

"So who's ready to plan a wedding?" Trisha asked. She walked into the room holding up her tablet. "I have some great ideas here I know you'll like, Jeff." Trisha sat down on the couch, looked at Jeff and patted the space next to her, urging him to sit.

When Haley gave Jeff an incredulous look, he kissed her quickly, got up, and headed for the kitchen. "I'll like whatever Haley likes, so you two plan away. I'm going to go find Steve and Kathy and those cookies. Have fun."

The look Haley gave him said she'd rather eat broken glass, but when she turned back to Trisha, she forced herself to smile. No matter how insane she thought this whole situation was, she knew right now she was stuck, and she had to make the best of it. She sat down next to Trish and looked at her tablet. "Okay, let's see what you have."

Trisha stood up. "Maybe we should wait for Jeff."

"No, I'm good," Haley said. "Like you said, we don't have a lot of time, so let's do this."

Trisha reluctantly sat down. "Okay. Here's what I'm thinking." She brought up some pictures on her tablet. "Here are some ideas I have for the cake, for the flowers, for the menu. I know Jeff doesn't like white cake, and he likes prime rib better than turkey, and Laura makes a great prime rib. For flowers, we're a bit limited, but I know Jeff likes red roses—he used to always get them for me. They're his favorite."

Haley gave Trisha a look like she had sprouted two heads, but Trisha didn't see it. She was too busy pulling up more pictures. Speechless, Haley looked over to Max lounging by the fire. He got up and trotted over to them.

At first it looked like he was going to sit by Trisha again, but then he changed his mind and sat down at Haley's feet instead. She instantly felt a rush of victory. She knew it was ridiculous to be jealous of Max also liking Trisha. As she petted him, she decided she could share Max, but there wasn't a snowball's chance in the desert she was going to share Jeff, and the sooner Trisha knew that, the better.

"So what do you think?" Trisha asked, finally looking up from her tablet.

Haley locked eyes with her. "I think you're still in love with my fiancé."

Trisha didn't even pretend to be shocked. She simply smiled and stared back at Haley. "I've always been in love with Jeff, and he was in love with me for many years. Jeff, Ben, Jeff's mom, this place, has been a big part of my life and always will be."

Haley just stared back at her. Trisha wasn't pulling any punches. She almost admired her for not trying to deny how she obviously still felt about Jeff. But this was a problem, a big problem. So Haley chose her words carefully, using the same words Jeff had said to her. "I understand Jeff was your past, but he's my future. We're together now, and we love each other very much." She paused a moment and waited for Trisha to say something, but when Trisha just kept flipping through pictures on her tablet, she continued. "I just want you to understand and respect that we're together now. We're getting married . . ."

Trisha looked up from the tablet. "Obviously, or Ben wouldn't have asked me to help plan your wedding. I don't want to let him down—he's done a lot for me over the years—so let me show you what I'm thinking for a menu, so we can get Laura started."

Haley couldn't tell if Trisha was being genuine or sarcastic. She didn't know what to say, so instead, confused, she looked down at the menu Trisha had pulled up on her tablet. The more Trisha talked about what appetizers they should have, the more surreal the whole thing felt to Haley. She was more than a little relieved when Kathy and Steve walked back in.

"So, how's the wedding planning going?" Kathy asked cheerfully.

"Great." Both Haley and Trisha answered at the same time. But the tones of their voices suggested differently.

Steve held up a platter of Christmas cookies. "Who needs a sugar break?"

Haley grabbed one and took a big bite.

Trisha waved them away. "I don't eat carbs."

Haley took another big bite of her cookie.

Steve put the cookies down. "I was going to head outside. Ben wanted me to check out some new Christmas lights he just put up before it gets dark. Trisha, you always had a great eye for decorations. Why don't you come with me? I could use your help."

Trisha's smile seemed forced. "Sure." She gave Haley her tablet. "Why don't you look over my ideas and let me know what you like, and we'll get this thing done."

As Trisha walked out of the room with Steve, Kathy turned to Haley. "We'll get this thing done? That doesn't sound very romantic or weddinglike to me. I'm sensing a little tension here."

"You think?" Haley shook her head, frustrated.

"If you don't want her here, just tell Jeff we can plan this wedding. It's not brain surgery."

"Oh sure, and then I look like the insecure jealous girlfriend who sent Trisha home after she came all the way up here, at Christmas, to help with the wedding. Ben apparently loves her. That's why he asked her to come. Even Max loves her. As long as Jeff doesn't love her, I can handle it."

Kathy gave her a sharp look. "You sure?"

Haley nodded, forced a smile. "Yes, I can be the bigger person, for Jeff and for Ben. But don't you think it's strange he never told me about her? They dated for five years."

Kathy looked surprised. "I really don't know. I don't know the whole story."

"That's the problem," Haley said. She looked worried. "Neither do I."

"If you have any doubts, just talk to Jeff. I know he's crazy about you."

Haley nodded, but still didn't look convinced.

Kathy sat down next to her. "Okay, then let's see what Trisha's thinking for the wedding. Does she have good ideas?"

Haley sighed. "Yeah, she's put together everything Jeff would want."

"But what do you want?"

Haley shook her head sadly. "I just want to marry Jeff, but honestly, I was really looking forward to wearing the dress, all the flowers, the cake. I know at first that didn't matter to me, but then I got all caught up in doing the pictures for my parents' B&B, and I guess I drank the wedding Kool-Aid. Now that it's gone, I want it back. I sound like Bridezilla, right?"

"No, of course not," Kathy said. "You have every right to be disappointed after everything that's happened. You're worried about your parents and the B&B, and now you come up here and you have to deal with Jeff's old girlfriend and start over planning a wedding when you have less than two days to do it. No, you're entitled to freak out a little. Bridezilla away. You've earned it."

Haley laughed. Kathy always had a way of making her feel better. "You're the best."

Kathy got up and walked over and picked up a Santa figurine. "I know."

They shared a laugh.

"But seriously," Kathy said, "we're up here at Christmas Camp, and this place is so magical. This is where you fell in love. Sure, your wedding is going to be different, but it can still be special."

"I agree," Jeff said as he entered the room.

When Haley stood up, Kathy gave her a quick hug. "I'm going to go catch up with Steve and Trisha and see if there's anything I can help with." Kathy turned to Jeff. "By the way, your friend Steve . . . what's his story? Is he single?"

"Kathy!" Haley playfully swatted her.

"What? He's hot. It's a fair question."

Jeff laughed. "He is single, but he's a tough one to pin down. He's always traveling with work."

"Well, he's here now," Kathy said as she headed out the door. "Let's see if I can catch him."

"Seriously?" Haley threw up her hands.

"I meant, catch up to him outside," Kathy said with a wink, before she left the room.

Jeff took the tablet from Haley. "So, let's plan our wedding."

Haley watched him flip through a couple of pages. "Wow, it looks like she has all my favorite things here."

"Uh-huh," Haley said. She sounded less than thrilled.

Jeff looked up immediately. "You're sure you're going to be okay with this?"

Ben entered the room. "Okay with what? Is there a problem?"

"Trisha," Jeff said. "Haley's a little uncomfortable with her planning our wedding."

Haley gave Jeff a look. She didn't want to look like the bad guy. "I was just thinking, there's not a lot to do since we're just having a simple ceremony. It doesn't make sense to have Trisha here when she should be home with her family at Christmas."

"That's the thing," Ben said. "Trisha doesn't have any family close by and usually spends Christmas up here with us, so she doesn't have to be alone."

Haley gave Jeff a surprised look. "So, even after you broke up, she still came up here for Christmas?"

Ben answered for him. "Yes. It's a tradition for her, except last year when she was traveling—that's why you didn't meet her. I thought this was a good thing. We have a last-minute wedding to plan and she's a wedding planner and was happy to help."

I bet, Haley thought.

Ben saw the look on Haley's face. "Is there a problem?"

Haley wanted to say that there was a huge problem. She wanted to tell Ben that Trisha obviously still had feelings for Jeff and that the way she kept looking at him made Haley very uneasy. She didn't trust her. She had wanted a small wedding with just close family and friends, and while Ben thought Trisha was a family friend, Haley wanted to say she was very nervous about just how friendly Trisha wanted to be with Jeff. But when she opened her mouth to express her concerns, she was stopped by the look on Ben's face. He was eagerly waiting for her response. She knew Ben would never intentionally do anything to hurt her and that he had asked for Trisha's help genuinely thinking he was doing her a favor.

"I wanted you to have a special wedding," Ben said. "I know how disappointed you are that you can't have it at your parents', so I thought Trisha could help make the best of things here since that's what she does for a living, and she's very good at it." Ben was starting to look concerned.

When Haley couldn't find her words, Jeff came to her rescue. "Haley's just a little uncomfortable knowing I dated Trisha . . ."

Ben gave Haley a surprised look. "But that was several years ago. That's water under the bridge, and you and Trisha remained good friends."

"We have," Jeff agreed. "But . . ."

Ben's shoulders slumped. He looked at Haley then back at Jeff. "But, I messed up. I'm really sorry, Haley. Everything happened so fast. I just wanted to help and thought Trisha could do that . . ."

Haley hated seeing Ben look so disappointed. She rushed over and gave him a hug. "It was very thoughtful of you. You're always trying to help and thinking about other people. That's what I love about you."

"But you want her to go?" Ben asked. He looked troubled. "I just don't think she has anywhere else to go now for Christmas . . . But you come first. Just tell me what you want me to do."

Jeff looked at Haley.

Haley forced herself to smile. As much as she wanted Trisha to go, she didn't want to disappoint or upset Jeff and Ben. They meant everything to her. So, if that meant she would have to put up with Trisha, she would do it.

"It wouldn't be right to ask her to leave now, so close to Christmas. She should just stay," Haley said.

"Are you sure?" Ben asked. "I can ask her to leave right now."

"No, I'm sure," Haley said and forced a smile for Ben's sake.

When Jeff gave her a concerned look, Haley nodded to let him know she was okay, but the truth was, she wasn't. She needed a moment to regroup.

"I think I'm going to run upstairs and freshen up," Haley said.

Jeff held up the tablet. "But what about the wedding plans?"

"You go ahead and look at everything. I'm sure whatever you want will be fine, and you know best what we can and can't do up here."

Jeff looked concerned. "Haley . . ."

She smiled back at him. "No, really, it's okay. At the end of the day, all I want to do is marry you. Whatever you want is fine with me." Haley gave him a quick kiss. "As long as you're standing next to me on Christmas Eve and we're getting married, I'll be happy."

"Are you sure?" Jeff asked, looking into her eyes.

She smiled but looked away quickly and started heading out of the room. "I'm sure."

"Okay," Jeff said. "I'll look at everything, and we can decide together later."

"Sounds good," Haley said and picked up her pace. She didn't want anyone to see she was crying.

Chapter Five

As HALEY ENTERED the all-white angel bedroom, the same room she had when she first came to Christmas Camp, she shut the door behind her and leaned against it. She impatiently brushed away her tears. She was mad at herself for getting so emotional. That wasn't like her. She wasn't usually the type to cry. The tears had just come out of nowhere. *Okay*, she thought, *maybe not nowhere.* In the last few hours, she had gone from planning a beautiful wedding that was also going to help launch her parents' new B&B business to having everything underwater at the B&B, moving the wedding at the last minute to Christmas Camp, and having Jeff's ex be the wedding planner.

She shut her eyes and took a deep breath to steady herself. When she opened them again, the first thing she saw was all the angel figurines staring back at her.

The angel room was decorated with dozens of different kinds of angels, from the angel figurines on the dresser and nightstands to the pictures on the wall and the pillows on the bed.

She smiled a little, remembering how they used to freak her out and how she'd hidden them all away the first time she'd stayed. But now as she looked at them, they felt like old friends and brought her comfort.

She had meant what she'd said to Jeff about the most important thing to her was marrying him, not the who, what, why, and where. She loved him. More than she had ever loved anyone before. But loving someone that much scared her. She couldn't imagine the pain of losing him. Hearing about Trisha and how they'd dated for five years had her feeling insecure for the first time about the relationship they'd built.

"This is crazy, right?" Haley said out loud. She was talking to the angels, as she started pacing around the room. "I know how much Jeff loves me. Trisha is his past. I'm just stressed and tired and overreacting." Haley stopped and looked at one of the pictures of an angel. "Good, you're not talking back, because if you were then I'd know I was really losing it."

Haley fell back onto the bed and closed her eyes. She told herself she just needed some rest, and then she'd feel better. But after a few minutes, when her mind refused to turn off, she opened her eyes, frustrated, and stared at the ceiling. She knew there was no way she could rest.

She got up and grabbed her laptop out of her bag and sat back down on her bed. Work was the one thing that always made her feel better. The one place she always felt safe and in control. She opened up a file that had photos of her parents' B&B and started scanning through them. When she looked up and saw the angels were staring at her, she gave them a look.

"What? I know I told Jeff I would take a break and not work while I'm here, but his old girlfriend also wasn't supposed to be my wedding planner, so it is what it is. I get a pass."

An hour later, Haley was still working when she heard a knock on her door.

"Come in," Haley said.

Kathy opened the door. "Ah, now I see why you're hiding out. You're working."

Haley closed her laptop. "I'm not hiding."

"But you are working? I thought you promised Jeff . . ."

Haley held up her hand to stop her. "Don't even say it. There were some things I needed to do."

Kathy sat down on the bed next to her. "Needed to do, or are you just working because that's what you do when you're upset and don't want to deal with something."

"You make it sound like working is a bad thing. It's what has made me so successful."

"And I thought you learned your lesson here last year at Christmas Camp that sometimes you just need to take a break and concentrate on what really matters most, and right now, that would be your wedding, Jeff, your friends, me, and your family. You know, the important stuff. With me being at the top of the list, of course."

Haley couldn't help but laugh. "Of course."

Kathy shut Haley's laptop, stood up, and grabbed Haley's hand and pulled her up, too. "Jeff and Ben sent me to come get you. Ben made a fresh batch of hot chocolate. He said it's your favorite."

Haley couldn't help but smile. "Everything they do up here is my favorite."

Kathy linked arms with her. "I'm beginning to see why."

As they walked out, arm in arm, Haley dropped her head to Kathy's shoulder. "Thanks."

"For what?"

"For being a good friend."

"Always."

When they came down the stairs, Jeff was waiting for them. He looked into Haley's eyes.

"All good?" he asked. He still looked concerned.

She smiled back at him and took his hand. "All good." When she said it, she really wanted to mean it more than anything in the world, but she was still worried, and what she hated most was that she wasn't sure what she could do about it.

As they walked into the kitchen, Jeff smiled at her, but when he looked up, his smile faded.

"What happened in here?" Jeff asked as he looked

around. "What are all these new decorations? And why do we have a Christmas tree in the kitchen?"

Ben grinned back at him. "Isn't it great? It was all Gail's idea. She brought some of her decorations from home and gave the kitchen a whole new look."

Jeff gave his dad an incredulous look. "But the kitchen didn't need a whole new look. Mom always had her special way to decorate in here, and where are all of Mom's poinsettias? I didn't see them when I came in. They're usually everywhere, in the living room, dining room, in here. They were her favorite. Where are they?"

Jeff, Haley, and Kathy all looked at Ben.

He smiled as he handed each of them hot chocolate.

When Jeff got his mug, he looked even more upset. "And what are these?" Jeff held up his mug. It was an adorable snowman mug. Jeff shook his head. "Where are the Santa mugs we always use?"

"We got some new mugs," Ben said. "Gail thought they'd go great with our Santa mugs. All the guests love them."

"They're adorable," Kathy said, but when Jeff gave her a look, she quickly stopped talking.

Jeff put down his mug without drinking anything. "I just don't understand why we need all these changes. Christmas Camp has always been about celebrating tradition, and we always do our traditional decorations. That's what the guests love and count on."

"But now we're adding some of Gail's traditions. It

means a lot to her, and the guests really do love it, too. It's always nice to start some new traditions, don't you think?"

But the look on Jeff's face said he didn't agree at all.

Haley took his hand. "I think it looks great. Sharing traditions is what Christmas Camp is all about, right?"

Trisha walked into the kitchen and looked around. "But it does look a lot different than what your mom always did."

Jeff let go of Haley's hand and pointed at Trisha. "Exactly."

When Haley saw Ben's disappointed look, she went and stood next to him. "I think there's always room for new traditions."

"I agree," Ben said.

Jeff clearly didn't. "So, where are the poinsettias? That's one of our oldest traditions."

"The thing about the poinsettias is they can be poisonous for cats, so we've been using Christmas lilies this year instead," Ben said. "Gail's going to bring some when she comes up tomorrow. Now that we'll be spending Christmas here."

Jeff gave his dad an incredulous look. "What are you talking about? We don't have a cat, and we always do Mom's poinsettias."

As if on cue, an adorable white fur ball of a cat with huge emerald-green eyes strutted into the kitchen and straight over to Jeff and rubbed up against Jeff's leg and meowed, Jeff gave his dad a stunned look.

"What is this?"

Ben chuckled as he picked up the pretty kitty and snuggled her. "This is Snowball. She's the newest addition to our family. I got her for Gail last month for her birthday. We found her at the same shelter we found Max." Ben held Snowball up to Jeff. "Do you want to hold her?"

"No." Jeff backed away. He looked overwhelmed. "I need some air." When he turned to leave, Trisha went to follow him.

Haley stopped her. "No, I'll go."

Ben looked worried. "I think he's really upset."

"It'll be okay. I'll give him a second and then go talk to him."

Ben nodded and cuddled Snowball. Haley petted Snowball, too.

Max came over and sat down at Ben's feet.

"So, how is Max with Snowball?" Haley asked.

Ben put Snowball down, and Max nuzzled her. "He loves her. I think he likes having a friend, and Snowball pretty much does her own thing. You know how cats are. So, she's usually hiding somewhere and doesn't take any of the attention away from Max. That's probably why he's okay with it."

Haley smiled and watched Max and Snowball sniff each other. "Well, I think she's a wonderful addition."

"Now I just need my son to think so," Ben said.

Haley nodded. "I'll go talk to him." She gave Ben a hug. "Don't worry—everything will be okay."

By the time Haley caught up with Jeff outside, he had one of the LED reindeer decorations upside down. He was adjusting its leg so it would stand up straighter. Haley knew when Jeff was upset he always had to fix something. Remembering the story of Jeff and his mom and the reindeer, Haley wasn't surprised to see Jeff working on the reindeer that had the makeshift red nose. She knew why he was so upset, and her heart ached for him.

"You okay?" she asked quietly.

"Yeah, just fixing this reindeer."

When Jeff didn't look up at her, she kneeled down next to him. When he finally looked at her, she could see the pain in his eyes.

"I know how much you miss her," Haley said.

Overwhelmed with emotion, he could only nod.

As they both stood up together, she gave him a hug and held on tight.

"It's going to be okay."

Jeff pulled back slowly. He looked up into the sky. "I know she's gone. It's been three years, and we all have to move on but . . ."

Haley took his hand. "But it's hard."

Jeff nodded. "You know I think Gail's great. I'm so glad my dad has someone to keep him company. It just seems like everything is happening so fast, so many changes. Did you see the cat? We have a cat!"

"It was a cute cat." Haley tried to lighten the mood.

"It was a cat!" Jeff said as he shook his head in disbelief. "I'm not a cat person."

"Maybe she'll grow on you."

"And who names a cat Snowball?" Jeff rolled his eyes.

"Someone who owns a Christmas Camp."

When Jeff couldn't help but laugh, Haley looked relieved. "Just talk to your dad. Tell him how you feel. He'll understand."

"That's hard to do when I don't even know how I feel. Does that make sense?"

Haley nodded. She understood only too well. That's how she felt about the Trisha situation. Christmas Camp had never felt so complicated.

As they walked back to the inn together, Haley kissed Jeff. "I love you."

Jeff gave her a look that was filled with love. "Love you, too." He looked up into the sky. It was just starting to get dark, and the first stars were showing up. "I wish you'd been able to meet my mom . . ."

Haley put her arm around him. "Me, too. But I really love what your dad always says, that the stars in the sky are the people we've loved and lost watching over us. I like to think your mom is doing that . . ."

They both looked up together at the sky.

Jeff nodded. "I'd like to think that, too."

A FEW HOURS later, as everyone—Ben, Jeff, Haley, Trisha, Steve, Kathy, and Laura—all gathered around the beautifully set dinner table, the mood was much lighter. There was laughter and joy, and looking around, Haley felt grateful. At that moment, she didn't even mind that Trisha was part of the group or that she had snagged the seat on the other side of Jeff. What was getting all of Haley's attention now was watching Kathy's and Steve's reaction to the remarkable meal Laura had prepared. Beyond her always-popular pot roast, Laura had also served roasted cauliflower with melted white cheddar cheese, Brussels sprouts with bacon, roasted baby potatoes, and tomato salad with feta.

"This meal is amazing," Kathy said. "I can't believe you put this all together so quickly not knowing any of us were going to be here."

Laura smiled as she passed the Brussels sprouts to Ben. "I'd already planned the pot roast for my family. It's always a dish we have this time of year, because it's easy to make and you have lots of leftovers."

"Except for tonight," Jeff said as he took a big slice of roast and put an equally big slice on Haley's plate for her. "You know your pot roast is one of my favorites."

Laura nodded. "And that's why I knew it was perfect for tonight. A pot roast is great comfort food. It's like serving a big, warm hug, and I thought you and Haley might be needing that tonight with everything that's happened today."

Kathy looked at Laura. "That is so sweet. That settles it. I'm never leaving here."

Everyone laughed.

"Thank you, Laura. I know we all appreciate this," Haley said and gave her a grateful look, "but what about your family? If we're eating your pot roast, what are they eating?"

"A pizza," Laura said. "I never let them order pizza. They're loving it."

Everyone laughed again.

When Haley tried to pass the potatoes to Trisha, Trisha shook her head. "No, thank you. I don't do carbs."

Instead, Trisha helped herself to some salad and smiled at Laura. "Thank you for making my favorite salad. I always look forward to it."

Haley fought to keep her smile on her face.

Kathy, seeing Haley struggling, held up her plate. "I'll take some potatoes. They look delicious, just like everything else. It's a good thing I'm only staying a few days here, or I'd be in trouble. I've already packed on a few pounds from overindulging at all the Christmas parties."

Steve gave Kathy an admiring look. "Well, whatever you're doing, it looks great on you."

Kathy, flattered, smiled back at him. "Flattery will get you everywhere."

Steve laughed and held up his wineglass. "That's what I'm hoping."

Haley watched as Kathy laughed and clinked her wineglass to Steve's. She knew that look on her best friend's face. Kathy was falling for Steve. She needed to find out Steve's story. She only knew what Jeff had told her about how he always traveled for work and never stayed in one place long enough to have a long-term relationship. She didn't want Kathy getting hurt, falling for someone who was unattainable.

Ben stood up and held up his wineglass. "Before we enjoy this lovely meal, I want to make a quick toast."

Jeff looked into Haley's eyes, and they shared a special smile, as they picked up their wineglasses together.

"First I want to thank you all for being here and everyone coming together at the last minute to make this wedding special for my son and soon-to-be daughter-in-law," Ben said. When Ben looked over at Jeff and Haley, Jeff gave Haley a quick kiss on the cheek. Haley looked over and saw Trisha was the only one not smiling. Ben continued, "We have a traditional toast we do at our Christmas Camp, and I thought it would be perfect for this occasion, as well. Son, will you help me?"

"Of course," Jeff said. He got up and went to stand over by his dad.

Both Jeff and Ben held up their glasses.

"To our family, friends, and community . . ." Ben looked at Jeff to continue the toast.

"To the people we've lost but will never forget . . ." Jeff looked back at his dad to finish.

"To love everlasting. Merry Christmas!" Ben said.

Everyone joined in the toast. "Merry Christmas."

As everyone toasted, Haley watched as Ben turned to Jeff. "We have so many wonderful traditions that we will always honor, like this one, and the ones we had with your mom. But I believe as we bring new people into our lives"—Ben looked over at Haley—"that we can also bring in new traditions."

Haley smiled back at them both. The two men she had come to love so much.

Jeff nodded and put his arm around his dad. "I think you're right, and I'm sorry for overreacting earlier. It just caught me off guard. You know I love Gail."

"And I do, too," Ben said. "We can talk more later, but I just wanted you to know how much I love you and the life we've built here and all our traditions that we'll always honor."

When Ben and Jeff hugged, Haley felt so relieved. She smiled at Jeff when he looked over and nodded her approval.

Once Jeff and Ben sat back down everyone started enjoying their dinner. After the meal was done, Laura got up and started clearing away the dishes until Ben and Jeff stopped her. Jeff took a plate from her. "You know the rules, Laura. You cook. You don't clean. We got this, don't we, Dad?"

Ben smiled at Laura. "We sure do, and thank you for another wonderful dinner."

"It really was fantastic," Kathy said.

Laura smiled. You could tell the compliments meant a lot to her. "Thank you, and there's dessert in the kitchen when you're ready. Fresh berry pie."

When Jeff quickly headed for the kitchen, Haley

grabbed his arm. "You can't seriously have room for that right now?"

"What?" Jeff tried to look innocent. "I'm putting the dishes away."

"Uh-huh." Haley laughed. "I know you, and I know you love berry pie."

"Not as much as I love you." Jeff gave her a quick kiss.

Kathy laughed. "Oh, he's good."

"Right?" Haley shook her head. "His sweet tooth is incredible."

Ben looked around the room. "You know what it's time for?"

Haley shook her head. "What?"

"Christmas Camp Charades!" Ben said, sounding excited. "Let me just finish cleaning up, and we can play."

Jeff laughed. "I think everyone's too tired tonight."

Ben looked disappointed.

"We should wait until everyone gets here," Haley said. "Then we can really have a great game."

"That's true. The more the merrier, and Gail does love the game. Okay, then tomorrow night."

Steve stood up from the table. "I'd love some dessert, but first I think I need to walk off some of this amazing meal." Steve patted his perfectly flat six-pack of a stomach. "Anyone want to join me?" Steve looked right at Kathy.

Kathy grinned back at him and stood up. "That sounds like a great idea."

"Anyone else?" Steve asked.

Haley was about to say something, but when Kathy gave her a look, she shut her mouth.

Kathy turned back to Steve. "Looks like it's just us."

"And I should be getting back to my family before they order a second pizza," Laura said.

Haley gave her a heartfelt hug. "Thank you so much for dinner tonight, and all you're doing for the wedding. I couldn't do this without you."

"Well, you could. You'd just be eating a lot of pizza," Laura said.

Haley laughed.

"And we really do need to decide the menu for the rehearsal dinner and the wedding first thing tomorrow morning, so we have a chance to shop for everything," Trisha said.

Laura smiled back at Trisha. "I'll be back tomorrow morning, and we'll figure it all out. But I agree, the sooner the better. Our little grocery store has a limited selection, and I'm sure right now a lot is probably sold out."

"I can always have my mom pick up whatever we need before they come up from Boston," Haley said.

Laura nodded. "That's an excellent idea. That will really help. Okay, sounds like we're all set. I'll see everyone in the morning."

"How far away do you live, Laura?" Kathy asked.

"I'm just a few miles away, right before the turnoff to the inn," Laura answered. "Very convenient. Just another reason why I love working here."

Trisha stood up. "I think I'm going to turn in," Trisha

said. "We have a lot to do tomorrow. Good night, everyone."

Everyone answered, "Good night."

When Haley started helping to pick up dishes, Ben stopped her. "It is going to be a big day tomorrow. Why don't you turn in, too? Jeff and I have this."

"Are you sure?" Haley asked.

Jeff came into the dining room, holding a plate, eating a piece of Laura's pie. "We're sure."

Haley couldn't help but laugh. She went over and kissed Jeff's cheek. "Behave yourself. Save some pie for the rest of us."

"Of course," Jeff said, feigning innocence. When Jeff held out a piece of pie for Haley to eat, she smiled and took the bite, and then laughing, she headed out of the room.

SEVERAL HOURS LATER, Haley was cozy in bed with her laptop, working on her parents' B&B website. Kathy was right. The website was looking really strong and even though the wedding pictures would have been a great addition, they weren't needed. The B&B impressed on its own.

She smiled at the picture of her parents, arm in arm, in front of the B&B. Their smiles were so welcoming and sincere. Haley knew that picture alone would draw people in. She couldn't wait to see them and everyone else tomorrow.

This wedding was really happening, but before it did, she still wanted and needed to talk to Jeff one more time about Trisha and make sure he really had moved on and was really ready to marry her. She knew she was being paranoid. He'd already explained everything to her, but for her own peace of mind, she had a few more questions she wanted to ask him before she could truly stop worrying. She knew it was going to be a big day tomorrow and the thing she needed the most right now was to get some sleep. She was exhausted.

After turning off the light and snuggling deeper under the covers, she smiled at one of the angel figurines that was glowing in the moonlight, before drifting off to sleep.

Chapter Six

HALEY WOKE UP to a familiar sound, a single, insistent bark from Max. She laughed as she got out of bed and opened her door. Max, wearing a red-and-green-striped Christmas sweater, trotted into the room, carrying his leash in his mouth. He dropped it at Haley's feet.

Haley gave him a look. "Are you up to your old tricks again? Did Jeff already walk you, and you're just trying to con me into another walk, like you always do?"

For an answer Max tilted his head and gave her his best innocent, adorable look. It worked. It always worked. Haley headed for the closet.

"Okay, Max, you win. Give me a second to get dressed. But it has to be a short walk. I have a wedding to plan today!"

WITH MAX HAPPILY walking along beside her, Haley opened the front door of the inn and was startled by the icy blast of cold air.

"Whoa, the temperature sure did drop." She wrapped her scarf tighter around her neck and hurried to keep up with Max, who was pulling at his leash, anxious for his walk. As she stepped outside, she looked up at the sky and saw thick, grey, low-level clouds. She looked at Max. "Let's make this quick. It looks like it's going to snow."

"I thought I might find you two out here."

Haley turned around smiling, as Jeff came out the front door. He walked over and gave her a kiss. "Good morning, beautiful."

Max barked and wagged his tail.

Haley laughed. "I think he was talking to me, Max."

Jeff petted Max. "But you're really cute, too." Jeff looked up at Haley. "Trisha's looking for you."

"Already? When did you see her?"

"She was up, already working, when I took Max for a walk earlier," Jeff said.

Haley looked surprised. She gave Max a look. "So, you already walked Max this morning? I thought he needed to go out."

Jeff laughed. "That's Max's favorite trick and looks like you fell for it."

"Seriously?" When Haley stared down at Max he just wagged his tail.

"She says you wanted to plan a menu and get some

things for your mom to pick up before they leave Boston and head up here today."

Haley sighed. "She's right. But before I go in, I wanted to talk to you about Trisha."

"Sure," Jeff said.

Haley took a deep breath, as they continued to walk Max together. "I know you've already explained everything, but we're getting married tomorrow, and I just want to make sure you don't have any doubts about us. I just keep wondering how you know for sure that I'm the one you want to spend the rest of your life with. You were with Trisha for five years, and like you said yourself, you didn't have a big fight or anything like that. You broke up because you were devastated about your mom's death. That's totally understandable, but it looks like she's been holding on to hope this whole time that someday, when the timing was better, you'd be able to get back together." Haley took a deep breath. "Did you ever really deal with the feelings you had for her?" She stopped to look up at him. "I'm sorry—it's just that all of this is what keeps going around in my head. We've always been able to talk about anything, so I want you to know, you can be honest with me now about this. I can handle it. I just need to know." Haley's voice wavered at the end. She was getting emotional again. The thought of losing Jeff terrified her. She believed he would never lie to her, but she worried he didn't really know his own feelings and that maybe deep down he still felt something for Trisha that he hadn't even realized yet.

Jeff stopped walking and without saying anything, put his arms around her, and gave her a hug. It made her feel safe and cared for, and she loved him even more for it.

When she looked up at him, he smiled at her. "Do you know one of the things I love most about you?" he asked.

She shook her head.

"I love that you always talk to me about how you feel. You don't just hold it all inside and expect me to read your mind. You come right out, like this, and ask me. Communication is everything in a relationship, and I think you and I do it really well."

Haley nodded. "I agree. I feel like everything is moving so fast, I just want to make sure you and I are okay. I know seeing Trisha was a surprise for you, too. How can you be sure you don't still have feelings for her?"

"I'll always care about her," Jeff said. "We have a history together, but I never felt about her the way I feel about you. When Trisha and I dated, we had a good relationship, but we never talked about getting married. Looking back, I'm not sure why. Maybe because we both had our careers, and we enjoyed each other's company, but we never had the kind of connection you and I have. Trisha will always matter to me. I truly see her as a friend, but even when we dated I never thought this is someone I can't live without and that's how I feel about you. You're my everything. You're the one I see spending the rest of my life with. I have no doubts. Not one.

There's a lot I don't know, but what I do know is that no matter what our future brings, as long as we're together, it will be okay. I love you, Haley. You've changed my life, and I can't wait to start building our life together."

Haley didn't even try to stop herself from crying this time, because these were tears of joy and gratitude. "I love you, too."

A light snow was just starting to fall when Jeff kissed her. It was one of those beautiful romantic moments Haley knew she'd remember for the rest of her life.

After they kissed, Haley gave Jeff another heartfelt hug. "Thanks for always making me feel like I can talk to you about anything. Even if it seems like I'm being crazy or I'm being insecure. Knowing you'll always listen makes me feel like together we can work anything out."

"I couldn't agree more," Jeff said. He gave her another quick kiss. "It's getting cold out here. Go inside. I'll take Max."

Haley smiled a brilliant smile. "This is really happening. We're getting married!" At this moment, she didn't even mind that she had to plan her wedding with Trisha.

Jeff smiled at her. "We sure are. Nothing can stop us."

"That's right!" Haley called over her shoulder as she hurried toward the inn. She was still smiling when she opened the front door and saw Trisha coming down the stairs. She was immaculately dressed, hair and makeup perfect.

"There you are," Trisha said. "When Jeff and I had breakfast together, I told him I was looking for you."

Haley looked surprised. "You two already had breakfast?"

Trisha nodded, smiled. "We were both up early and were starving so Jeff made one of his famous omelets. You know the ones with the mushrooms and sautéed peppers. They're my favorite."

Haley smiled back. "Mine, too." Now that she felt confident about Jeff's feelings for her, she actually felt a little sorry for Trisha. She continued up the stairs. "I'm just going to take a quick shower and see if Kathy's up. I want her input on the menu, and we'll be back down, and we can get everything all set."

"The sooner, the better," Trisha said.

"Agreed." Haley hurried up the stairs and was heading to her room when she ran into a tired-looking Kathy coming out of her room wearing her robe.

"Late night?" Haley asked.

Kathy yawned and then smiled. "Steve and I actually stayed up late watching old Christmas movies. I think I went to bed around three."

"You and Steve, huh?" Haley gave her a look.

Kathy smiled back at her, she looked happy, really happy. "He's a great guy."

"You just met him."

"But when you know, you know, right?" Kathy asked. "Plus, he's Jeff's best friend so he has to be great."

"You've spent more time with him than I have,"

Haley said. "But he does seem like a good guy. Still, be careful. I know how fast you can fall."

Kathy put her arm around Haley. "Don't worry. I have a good feeling about this one."

"Okay, but right now I need your help," Haley said. "Our wedding planner is downstairs, and she has us on a very tight schedule. So, take a quick shower and meet me downstairs in twenty minutes."

AN HOUR AND a half later, all three girls were getting up from the kitchen table. Everyone looked pleased.

"I think the menu for tonight's rehearsal dinner and tomorrow for the wedding is going to work out great," Haley said. "Thanks for all the help."

"We just need to make sure to get all the ingredients," Trisha said and handed Haley a sheet of paper. "Here's the list for your mom. There's a lot on it, but Laura's right, the store up here doesn't have much."

Haley took the list. "I'm on it. I'll call her right now. She's standing by."

"When are they heading up here?" Kathy asked.

"They said the plumbers were just finishing cleaning everything up, so they should be able to take off about noon."

"Perfect," Trisha said. "And when is everyone else coming?"

"Jeff said the rest of the gang are also heading up this

afternoon," Haley said. "So, by tonight, we should have a full house. It's going to be so great to see everyone."

Trisha looked at her tablet and frowned. "We have a lot to do before everyone gets here."

Laura walked in, overhearing the last of the conversation. "Then I'd say, it's time we divide and conquer." She took the list from Haley. "I can call your mom and give her the list. Because I'm making the meals, I can answer any questions she might have."

Haley gave Laura a grateful look. "That would be great. Thank you."

"Okay, let's go down the rest of our checklist," Trisha said. "Who has the rings?"

"My dad does. They had to be sized. He's picking them up today," Haley said.

"Great." Trisha marked another thing off her list. "And Ben said your dad is also going to officiate the wedding?"

Haley smiled. "He is, and he's very excited about it. He took the online course last year, so they could hold weddings at the B&B and he could officiate if someone wanted him to. But I'll be the first one he has done."

"That's so sweet," Kathy said.

"Well, I hope he's practicing," Trisha said. She looked worried.

Haley laughed. "Don't worry. He is. It'll be fine."

Trisha looked back at her tablet. "Okay, who is bringing the flowers?"

Haley and Kathy looked at each other.

"The flowers died in the flood," Haley said.

"It wasn't pretty," Kathy added.

Jeff walked into the kitchen. "What are you girls up to?" He headed straight for a cupboard, took out a pretty Christmas tin, opened it up, and took out one of the famous Christmas Camp sugar cookies.

"There they are!" Haley hurried over and took one. She smiled up at Jeff as she took a bite.

Kathy laughed. "Does Laura really hide them?"

Jeff and Haley, still chewing their cookies, nodded.

"I guess she would have to," Kathy said. "Hand one over." Kathy took a cookie. "Trisha, do you want one?"

"She doesn't do carbs, right?" Haley said.

"Right," Trisha answered. "Okay, we need to get back to work."

"How's the wedding planning coming along?" Jeff asked. "Did you see Dad's inspirational word for the day?" He pointed over to the chalkboard where Ben always did a Christmas countdown. Right now the chalkboard said *2 Days to Christmas* and the inspirational word for the day was *Devotion*.

"Devotion," Trisha said. "That's perfect because I'm devoted to making this wedding actually happen in the next twenty-four hours." She looked back at her tablet. "So who's bringing the flowers?" Trisha looked at Haley then at Jeff.

"Uh, no one," Haley said. "There wasn't any time to get any flowers."

Trisha looked horrified. "You can't have a wedding without flowers."

"Actually, you can," Haley said. "It's not that big of a deal."

"Well, flowers are kind of a big deal," Kathy said.

Haley gave her a look. "Whose side are you on?"

Kathy laughed. "The flowers' side?"

Trisha looked at Jeff. He looked at Haley.

"Flowers would be nice," he said. "We usually have all the poinsettias my mother loved, but now we don't have anything . . ."

Haley felt bad.

"Hold on. Let me see what I can do." Trisha left the room.

Stress eating, Haley grabbed another cookie from the tin and took a big bite.

"What happened to that sugar detox you were doing?" Kathy asked.

Haley laughed. "Oh, that was so last year."

Jeff laughed. "Thank goodness you gave that up."

When Trisha came back into the kitchen, she had a smug smile on her face. "Haley, we need to go."

"Where?" Haley asked.

"To get you some flowers. I called the flower shop in town. They think they might be able to help us figure something out. But we have to go now."

"Okay, let's go," Kathy said.

"Actually, Kathy, I have you going with Laura to get groceries, and Jeff, you need to work with your dad on those decorations we were talking about, and every-one needs to meet back here in two hours so we can go through the rest of the list."

"Decorations? What decorations?" Haley asked.

Jeff kissed her on the cheek. "It's a surprise. I gotta get going. I'll see you later. Good luck."

"You, too," Haley called out as he left the kitchen. She looked at Kathy. "Are you good with helping Laura?"

"Absolutely. Whatever you need."

"Great, then let's go," Trisha said, looking at Haley. "They're waiting for us."

"Wait, I have a question," Kathy said. "What about a photographer? I think that's even more important than flowers. The pictures you take you have for the rest of your life. The photographer we had in Boston couldn't make the trip up here."

"It's okay," Haley said. "We can just get some pictures with our phones. My mom's bringing up her camera. We'll make it work."

"We will do better than just make it work," Trisha said. "I've already found a photographer for you."

Haley looked amazed. "How did you do that? At the last minute. At Christmas?"

"He's a friend of mine," Trisha said. "Curt's parents have a place up here, not too far away, and he said he'd stop by on Christmas Eve and take some pictures as a favor to me. He is an excellent photographer."

Haley smiled at Trisha. "Thank you so much. That's so great. I really appreciate it."

Trisha nodded. "I know how much Jeff and Ben love pictures."

"And my family does, too," Haley said. "My mom still has pictures of her great-grandmother's wedding."

"We really do need to go," Trisha said.

"Okay, let's go," Haley said. "See you in a few hours, Kathy, and make sure Laura has enough ingredients to make some more Christmas cookies. In case Jeff has found her other hiding places."

Kathy laughed. "I'm on it."

THE LITTLE FLOWER shop in town, Petal Dreams, was as cute as its name. Out front, there was a stand next to the door with pretty pink, white, and red poinsettias, and gorgeous wreaths made out of fresh tree branches, holly, and pinecones. In the window, there was a cascade of white and silver stars, in different shapes and sizes. They twinkled when they caught the light.

Haley stopped to admire them as Trisha breezed into the shop.

"Haley, come on," Trisha called over her shoulder.

Haley quickly followed Trisha inside.

As soon as they entered, a man in his sixties, with a joyful smile, greeted them. Haley was surprised to see him give Trisha a hug.

"Trisha, it is so good to see you," the man said. He smiled at Haley. "Merry Christmas. You must be the bride."

Haley smiled back at him. "I am. Merry Christmas, and thanks again for helping us."

"Haley, this is Toby. Toby and his wife, Betty, have owned this flower shop for . . . how many years is it now, Toby?"

"Forty-three years." Toby beamed back at them. "Betty's in the back getting what we have left ready for you to see."

Haley looked around in awe at all the beautiful flower arrangements. She started to get really excited. She couldn't believe that such a tiny flower shop, tucked away up in the woods, could have so much. "Your selection here is amazing. I don't know what half these flowers are, but I know I love them all."

Toby looked pleased by the compliment. He happily guided her over to the roses. "Now, I know you know what these are. Our red roses and their connection to love are always a favorite choice at Christmas, and for weddings, our white roses are always popular, as they traditionally signify new beginnings."

Haley nodded, intrigued. "I didn't know that about white roses."

Toby continued walking her around and proudly pointed out different flowers. They all were in a deep rich Christmassy hue. "Also popular at Christmas are our dahlias, our ranunculus, and the amaranthus."

Haley laughed. "I can't even say half of those, but I love them all . . ." Haley's voice trailed off when she saw a stunning display of peonies and walked quickly toward it. "Now, these I know. I love peonies, but I've never seen them in this color."

Toby joined her. "These are called Red Charm Peonies. They're known for their rich burgundy color."

Haley looked over at Trisha, who was eyeing the red roses. "Trisha, I think these peonies would be perfect for the wedding. They're so beautiful and this color is the same color Kathy and my mom will be wearing."

Trisha held up a red rose. "But red roses are Jeff's favorite."

Haley fought to keep the smile on her face. "I'm sure he'll love these, too." But when Haley turned back to Toby, she saw the regretful look on his face.

"I'm afraid I don't have any peonies left. Or any red roses, or any of the flowers out here," Toby said.

"What do you mean?" Trisha asked. "You have so many."

Toby picked up the red roses Trisha was looking at and moved them over to the counter. "Unfortunately, they're all spoken for. We have a lot of Christmas Eve and Christmas parties and some weddings. Everyone is coming by today to pick up their orders for their big events. So everything you see here has already been sold."

Haley felt a crush of disappointment. "So, you don't have any of the peonies left? What about paperwhites? They're always so pretty at Christmas."

Toby shook his head. "No, I'm sorry. We hardly have any flowers left at all. We had to make an emergency run into Boston to get enough to finish one of our orders when they called last minute and ordered more table settings for a wedding. We got several last-minute rush orders that we weren't prepared for."

"Like us," Trisha said.

"But we only need a few flowers," Haley said. "I'm having a very small ceremony and usually there are poinsettias all around the house, but . . ."

Toby nodded. "I know. Ben usually orders them from me, but not this year."

"It's Snowball's fault," Haley said.

"Snowball?" Toby looked confused.

"The new cat," Trisha said.

Toby laughed. "Well, then that explains it. Gail has come in several times to get some Christmas lilies but she never mentioned Snowball. That's a cute name."

"It's a cute cat," Haley said.

Trisha checked the time on her phone. "We're on a tight schedule. You said you had put some things in the back for us?"

"Yes, come with me," Toby said. "I'll show you what we have."

Haley and Trisha followed Toby to the back room where his pretty and petite wife, Betty, was waiting with some greenery laid out on a table.

"Trisha, you remember, Betty, my wife," Toby said.

"Of course I do," Trisha said. "So good to see you, Betty. This is Jeff's fiancée, Haley."

Betty looked confused. "Your old boyfriend, Jeff? Ben's son?"

Trisha smiled. "Yes."

"And you're planning their wedding?" Betty gave Haley a surprised look.

Haley laughed. "Trust me. This wedding has been full of surprises. I'm thankful for Trisha's help and for yours with the flowers. Your shop is lovely. I'll be back when I have more time to spend."

"Thank you." Betty beamed back at her. "I wish we had more for you to choose from today, but I'm sure Toby told you, we're out of almost everything. But I had an idea for you."

Trisha walked up to see what Betty had laid out. "We're listening."

"I know you're getting married at Ben's place, where he does his Christmas Camps."

"That's right," Haley said.

"I've heard one of the activities they have you do is to go out in nature and create ornaments out of what you find," Betty said.

Haley smiled. "That's right. You are supposed to pick things that inspire you. Everyone loves that activity."

Betty picked up some Douglas fir branches and some holly branches from the table. "So, I thought what you might like to do for your bridal bouquet is use that inspiration and go gather things like this, from around the inn, like you do with the activity." Betty gathered up the branches, the holly with the red berries, and some other evergreens, and held them all together. "You then just need to tie a string at the top and bottom really tight to keep everything together and use some burlap ribbon like this to cover the stems and make a bow if you like." Betty held up her creation. It was beautiful.

Haley held her hand to her heart. "I love it. It's perfect. It will really mean something to everyone, and I know Jeff will love it, too."

"But it's not flowers," Trisha said, frowning.

"But it doesn't have to be flowers. I love that it can be anything that inspires us from nature. This way it will really mean something to us," Haley said and turned back to Betty. "But I know we don't have all of this at the inn—like holly."

Betty smiled. "We have some extra holly that we can spare. See how the holly has all the beautiful bright shiny red berries? They'll be perfect to add that pop of red. Just be careful, it's prickly. You only need a couple of branches to really make an impact. The main filler is Douglas fir branches, and I know you have a lot of those by the inn. You can use some other evergreens as well, like Balsam fir, if you want some variety." Betty picked up some green floral foam and a plastic tray. "Then you can also easily make some centerpieces by covering this foam with the Douglas fir branches and adding in some holly and anything else you like. You can put it in a container or a wicker basket."

Trisha nodded. She was quickly writing down notes

in her tablet. "We have the wicker baskets Ben always uses for the Christmas Camp when people gather ingredients for their ornaments, so we can use some of those, and I've made some centerpieces. So I'm sure I can pull something together."

"That would be great," Haley said. "Thank you so much, everyone."

Betty walked over to the flower cooler and opened the door and took out one dozen perfect pristine white roses. "These are the last roses we have. We were going to use them for our own Christmas centerpiece, but we would like to give them to you for your wedding," Betty said.

Haley looked touched. "Oh no, I couldn't take your roses."

"Please, we insist," Toby said. "We know how much joy flowers bring. It's why we do what we do, and we would really like you to have these for your wedding."

Betty came over and took one of the roses and put it in Haley's bouquet. "See, even adding one or two roses can really make a difference, and with the white roses signifying new beginnings, I think they are perfect for your wedding."

Haley nodded and gave Toby and Betty a grateful look. "They are perfect. This is so kind of you. Thank you so much."

Toby smiled back at Haley. "It's our pleasure. Merry Christmas."

Haley smelled her white roses and smiled back. "Merry Christmas."

Chapter Seven

As Haley and Trisha drove up to the inn, they saw the guys taking some Christmas lights to the backyard.

"Does this have something to do with my surprise?" Haley asked Trisha.

Trisha just shrugged.

Haley shivered as she got out of the car. The temperatures were really dropping, and the light snow that had started earlier was starting to pick up. When they opened the door and stepped inside, Snowball zipped by them. "I still can't get used to seeing a cat here," Haley said.

"Let's go see how Laura and Kathy did," Trisha said. Haley followed her into the kitchen where Laura was just putting out two pizza boxes.

"What is this?" Haley asked, laughing. "Pizza? No? We've never had pizza here."

"And we've also never planned a wedding in forty-eight hours," Laura laughed. "I'm making an exception. I know everyone's hungry, and I need time to start preparing our rehearsal dinner for tonight and making some of the hors d'oeuvres for the wedding tomorrow." Laura opened the pizza boxes. "So we have pepperoni and sausage and Canadian bacon and pineapple."

"That's Jeff's favorite and mine," Haley said.

Laura nodded. "I know, and it's your wedding, so we had to have your favorite."

Haley looked concerned. She came over and took Laura's hand. "This all sounds like way too much. Honestly, we don't need a cake or anything fancy. We could have pizza at my wedding for all I care. As long as we're all together."

Laura smiled and gave her hand a reassuring squeeze. "Now, don't you worry about a thing. You know I'm used to making big meals every night, and this time, I have all this help coming. Your mom said she's ready to pitch in, and so are Gail and Susie."

"And I'll help," Kathy said.

Haley laughed. "You don't cook! I think the best way you can help is stay out of the kitchen."

Kathy laughed. "Look who's talking."

"I agree," Haley said. "That's why you won't see me in here. I'm going to leave this to the pros or we will be ordering pizza."

Laura laughed. "Nobody's going to be ordering any more pizza after today."

Haley gave Laura a heartfelt hug. "You really are the best. I love you."

"I love you, too, sweetie. Now grab a slice of pizza before the guys get in here, and it disappears."

Haley laughed.

Laura went over to the refrigerator and took out a salad and gave it to Trisha. "I whipped up a quick salad for you. I know you don't eat pizza."

Trisha smiled. "Thank you, Laura. That's very sweet."

"Who doesn't eat pizza?" Steve said as he, Jeff, and Ben walked into the kitchen. "Trisha, you don't know what you're missing."

Trisha held up her salad. "I'm good. I have my salad."

Jeff came over and put his arm around Haley. "How did the flower trip go?"

Haley smiled a brilliant smile. "Amazing."

"What did you get?" Jeff asked. "Let's see."

Haley shook her head. "Nope, it's going to be a surprise. We're going to put everything together when the rest of the gang gets here, but there is something you guys can do for me."

"Whatever you need," Ben said.

"You know the wicker baskets you use for Christmas Camp? If you would fill several of those with some Douglas fir branches that are around twelve to fourteen inches long, that would be perfect."

Jeff looked intrigued.

"Consider it done," Ben said. "We can go get some right after lunch."

Trisha checked the time on her phone again. "Haley, we need to wrap up here to stay on schedule."

Haley took a big bite of her pizza. "What's left? I think we've done everything until the rest of the group gets here."

Trisha shook her head. "I need to see what you're both wearing so I can tell our photographer what to expect."

"I brought the tux I was planning to wear and a suit. I wasn't sure what would be best," Jeff said.

Trisha and Haley spoke at the same time.

"The suit," Haley said.

"The tux," Trisha said.

Haley laughed. "You were only wearing the tux before for the photos for the B&B. I don't even know if you need to wear a suit with a tie and all that for this wedding. This is just going to be a simple ceremony."

Trisha looked appalled. "This is a wedding not a barbecue. This is one of the most important moments in your life, and it's going to be photographed. You're going to have those photographs forever."

"I have to agree with Trisha on this one," Jeff said. "I want to look my best for you. It's our wedding, and you said you had an amazing dress. So, I'm thinking I need to wear the tux."

Haley's shoulders slumped. "Had a dress. I don't have it anymore."

"What do you mean?" Trisha asked. "What happened to your dress?"

"Nothing happened to it. I'm sure it's perfectly fine hanging back up at the boutique in Boston. I was doing a trade with them. They were giving me the dress for all the publicity photos we were doing, and I was going to give them some, as well, for their own advertising. But all that got canceled, so I had to give back the dress."

Trisha looked so upset you'd think she was the one getting married. "So, what did you bring to wear?"

Haley cringed. She had no idea this was going to be such a big deal. Seeing the way everyone was looking at her made her regret her next words. "I brought some black pants and a nice top."

"No, I meant, what did you bring to wear for the wedding?" Trisha asked impatiently.

Haley looked at Jeff before looking back to Trisha. "That's it. That's what I brought for the wedding. I was in a hurry and still upset and not even sure what we would be able to do up here, so I just grabbed something I thought would work."

The room was silent.

By the look on everyone's faces, Haley knew she had really messed up. "Okay, maybe I should have brought a dress. I was just thinking we were going to be up here in the woods. Pants seemed more practical. They're nice pants, designer . . ."

More silence.

Ben walked over and put his arm around Haley. "It's okay. I have an idea."

A FEW MINUTES later, Ben, Haley, Trisha, and Kathy were all upstairs in Ben's bedroom. He was holding a white garment bag.

"My wife, Grace, was very sentimental," Ben said. "She never could give away her wedding dress, and while I donated most of her clothes to charity, I just couldn't part with this." Reverently, he handed it to Haley. "I know she would want you to have it."

Haley looked overwhelmed with emotion.

Kathy had tears in her own eyes.

"But, I couldn't . . ." Haley said. She was at a loss for words.

Ben smiled. "You don't have to wear it if you don't want to, but I would like you to have it. Grace would have loved you so much, just like I do." Ben kissed Haley on the cheek and left the room.

Haley turned to Kathy. "I don't know what to say."

Trisha took the dress from her. "Let's see the dress."

Kathy took it back from Trisha and gave it to Haley. "It's Haley's dress. She can decide what to do with it."

"It seems pretty simple to me. You need a dress. Here's a dress. Let's see if it fits. You two are about the same size," Trisha said.

Haley nodded. "I know. Jeff let me wear some of her clothes the first time I came to Christmas Camp and hadn't packed properly. But a wedding dress is a whole different story, and I don't know if wearing Jeff's mom's dress is the right thing to do . . ."

"I think it's absolutely the right thing to do," Trisha said. "This way you would be honoring his mother's memory, and she would be part of the wedding. I know that would mean a lot to Ben, too."

Kathy nodded. "I think she's right. I think it would be really special. But only you can decide what's right for you."

Trisha eyed the garment bag. "So? Why don't you look at the dress and then you can decide. I need to go check with the guys about the decorations. Let me know what you decide." Trisha left the room.

Once she was gone, Haley turned to Kathy. "I don't know what to do."

Kathy put her arm around her. "Take a deep breath. It's all going to be okay. Let's just look at the dress and see what you think. Okay?"

Haley took a deep breath and nodded slowly. "Okay." Her hands trembled as she slowly unzipped the bag and carefully took out a lovely classic satin sheath wedding dress. It had a simple scoop neck and long sleeves. Haley caught her breath when she saw it and fought back tears. "It's perfect," she whispered, holding the dress up to her. She looked at Kathy.

The tears were back in Kathy's eyes. "It sure is," Kathy said. "Try it on. See how it fits." When Kathy took the dress from her, Haley quickly slipped out of her clothes and carefully, with Kathy's help, put on the dress.

Amazed, Kathy stood back and looked at her. "I can't believe it. It fits like it was made for you."

Haley didn't look surprised at all. She looked grateful. "Or like it was meant to be."

Kathy nodded. "Exactly."

Haley took a deep breath and smiled. "Everything's finally all coming together. I have flowers. I have a photographer, a dress. This wedding is really going to work . . ."

"Wait, don't say that, you might jinx . . ." But the rest of what Kathy was about to say was cut off by Trisha yelling up to them from downstairs.

"Haley!" Trisha hollered. "You need to come down here right away!"

HALEY WAS SMILING and humming the Christmas song *We Wish You a Merry Christmas* with Kathy as they headed down the stairs, but when they got to the bottom and saw everyone gathered in the sitting room looking concerned, Haley stopped singing.

"What's wrong?" she asked.

Jeff came over and took both her hands. "There's really no good way to tell you this, so I'm just going to give it to you straight."

"Okay, now you're starting to really scare me," Haley said. "Is everyone okay?"

Jeff nodded. "Everyone's fine, but a weather system has moved in. We thought it was going to miss us, but it changed course, and we're getting a direct hit now. The snow is coming down hard, and it's supposed to last for several days."

"But it was fine earlier," Haley said. "It wasn't snowing that much." Haley walked over to the window and looked out. She was stunned. The snow was now coming down so hard all she could see was a whiteout.

Jeff joined her. "They've just closed Alpine Road and some other roads as a precaution."

"But Alpine Road is the only way to get here," Haley said. When Jeff nodded, it hit her full force. "So, this means no one can get here for the wedding—my parents, Gail, everyone from Christmas Camp . . ."

"Or Laura," Ben added. "Thankfully, she left earlier right after lunch to get some things from home, but she won't be able to get back here now."

"And our wedding photographer won't be able to get here either," Trisha said. She looked as upset as Haley. "And your parents were bringing most of the food, the wedding rings, and your dad was officiating."

Haley nodded. She was still struggling to comprehend what was happening.

"So, what does this mean?" Kathy asked.

Haley, heartbroken, looked at Jeff. "It means we have to cancel the wedding. Again."

Chapter Eight

HALEY NUMBLY LEFT the group and walked over to the front door. When she opened it, a blast of wind and snow hit her full force, but she didn't flinch. She just kept staring out into the bleakness. She couldn't see more than a few inches in front of her, but that didn't stop her from taking a few more steps outside. "Why is this happening?" she whispered as more blinding snow hit her in the face.

Jeff quickly joined her, grabbed her hand, and pulled her back inside and shut the door. "Haley, come on. You can't go out there."

Haley laughed. It was the kind of laugh you heard right before someone lost it. "I can't go outside. I can't have my wedding. What else can't I do? I can't do anything. We can't do anything. This is . . ."

When Jeff took her into his arms, she finally calmed down, but with the calm came more pain. When she looked up, there were tears in her eyes. "I just wanted to marry you. This shouldn't be that hard . . ."

Jeff nodded. "I know."

"So, what do we do now?" Haley asked. "We were supposed to get married tomorrow, Christmas Eve . . ."

"We find another time," Jeff said. "We reschedule."

Haley looked brokenhearted. "But it meant so much to us, to all of us, to get married at Christmas, when we first met and fell in love . . ."

"Are you saying you want to wait until next Christmas?" Jeff asked.

"No. I mean, I don't know." Haley looked confused. "I don't know about any of this."

"Let's not make any decisions right now," Jeff said. "We should be grateful no one's stuck in this storm. Everyone's home safe. We're all here together. It's almost Christmas. Let's make the best of it."

Haley nodded. It was just another reason she loved Jeff so much. He was always looking at the positive side of things and didn't usually let stress get to him.

When there was a loud knock on the door, they both looked startled. Jeff immediately opened it and found Gail standing there covered in snow.

"Merry Christmas," she said, brushing snow off her.

Jeff pulled her quickly inside. "What are you doing here? How did you get here? Are you okay? Dad, Gail's here."

Ben came rushing over and gave her a hug. "I was so

worried about you. I've been calling and calling but no answer. I knew you weren't going to leave Boston until later, and I left you a message about the storm, but when I couldn't reach you I got worried."

Gail kissed his cheek. "I'm sorry I worried you. I wanted to surprise you all, so I left really early this morning and luckily I was almost here when the snow really hit. They closed the road behind me."

Haley gave Gail a hug. "I'm so glad you're okay."

Jeff hugged her, too. "We all are."

Snowball came running over to her. Gail picked her up and cuddled her. "There's my little Snowball." She handed Snowball to Ben. "But right now I'd just really like to get out of these wet clothes." She headed for the stairs. "I'll be back down soon."

"I'll make you some hot chocolate," Ben said.

"That sounds perfect," Gail said, smiling back at him.

A HALF HOUR later, they were all gathered in the kitchen. Haley watched as Gail helped Ben make the hot chocolate. They were so cute together. You could see how much they cared for each other. Haley looked over and saw that Jeff was watching them, too, and he was smiling. When Gail went to get out the mugs, she only took out the Santa mugs. Haley watched her exchange a look with Ben and saw that Jeff saw the look, too.

Jeff walked over to Gail and gave her another hug. "I'm

so glad you're here." He reached up into the cupboard and took out one of Gail's new snowman mugs. "I'd like to try one of these mugs. Seems perfect on a snowy day like this."

Gail touched Jeff's hand. "Are you sure? The Santa mugs are a tradition."

Jeff nodded. "And I say it's time we start making a new tradition with these snowmen."

Haley walked over and joined them and took out a snowman mug, too. "I agree."

Gail looked touched. "Thank you."

Haley knew Gail was thanking them for much more than just using the mugs.

Jeff smiled back at her. "You're welcome."

Just as they clinked snowman mugs together, the lights went out.

Haley laughed. "Seriously?"

Kathy laughed, too, and looked over at Haley. "What did you say to jinx us this time?"

Haley shook her head. "I swear I didn't say anything."

Ben tried the light switch but got nothing. "The power's out. It must be the storm." He opened a drawer and took out some flashlights and passed them around. "I'm going to go check on the generator. I don't hear it kicking in."

"I'll come with you," Jeff said.

A FEW MINUTES later when the guys returned Ben had a smile on his face. "So I have some good news and some bad news. What do you want first?"

"The bad news," Haley said.

"The bad news is the generator isn't working."

"And the good news?" Haley asked.

Ben grinned back at them all. "Now we can play Christmas Camp Charades."

Everyone laughed.

"Nice try, Dad," Jeff said.

Ben smiled back at him. "I'm serious. Who wants to play?"

"I do!" Kathy said. "I love games."

"Me, too," Steve chimed in. "But exactly what is this?"

Haley laughed at their enthusiasm. "It's something Ben does at all the Christmas Camps. It's like charades, only we play using Christmas songs, and you split into two teams. Each team gets a different song, and you compete at the same time. The first team to guess right, wins. It's hilarious."

Gail laughed. "Especially when you're wearing the crazy Christmas sweaters."

"Oh, that's right," Haley said. "How could I forget that part? Luckily, we don't have the sweaters this year."

Ben's smile grew. "Want to bet?"

AND A FEW minutes later everyone was wearing one of Ben's crazy Christmas sweaters, because of course, he had a collection of them, and they were playing Christmas Camp Charades. There was a lot of joking around and laughter, and once again, Haley ruled, winning her round against Jeff. The song she had gotten was Dean Martin's *Let It Snow, Let It Snow, Let It Snow*. For her clue, she had run outside and scooped up a bunch of snow and brought it in and dumped it on Jeff's head. By the time the game was over, Haley had laughed so much her stomach hurt. The crazy Christmas Camp Charades was exactly what she had needed to take her mind off of having to cancel her wedding for the second time.

AFTER CHARADES, BEN had another game for them to play that was all about how to make dinner without the groceries Haley's parents were bringing and without any electricity. It became a scavenger hunt through the kitchen where anyone who found something that could work would put it on the counter. Haley was rummaging through the pantry when Steve joined her.

He picked up a box of crackers. "How about these?" he asked.

"Sure," Haley said. "I saw some different cheeses and things in the refrigerator that Laura was going to use to make appetizers, so we can always do cheese and crackers."

"I'm pretty good at whipping things together," Steve said. "I'll go take a look at what we have."

Steve was about to leave when Haley stopped him. "Hey, I've been meaning to talk to you about something."

"Sure," Steve said. "What about?"

"Kathy."

Steve nodded, laughed a little. "Okay."

Haley chose her words carefully. "I've noticed you two hanging out a lot and you seem to be getting along well."

"We are. She's really great."

"She is," Haley said. "Look, I'm just going to say it. Jeff told me you traveled a lot. You're not one to really stay in one place for very long . . ."

"That's true," Steve said.

"So, how does that work with your relationships?"

"You mean, how would that work with Kathy."

"Yes," Haley said. "That's exactly what I mean. I just don't want to see her get hurt. I'm not saying you would do that intentionally. She just seems to really like you . . ."

"She's great. We're talking about maybe hanging out for Christmas Eve while I'm in town and then I guess we'll see."

Haley nodded. "Sorry if I seem a little overprotective . . ."

"You just care about your friend," Steve said. "I get it. All I can tell you right now is that Kathy is someone I want to get to know better and I'm not leading her on or anything like that. I would never do that."

"And now I see why you're Jeff's best friend," Haley said. She smiled. "Thanks for this little talk."

"Anytime." Steve grinned back at her. "But now I better go see what Laura has in the refrigerator to make us something to eat and I'm going to put as much as I can into the freezer. Even with the power out the freezer will keep things cold for forty-eight hours if you don't open it again."

LATER THAT NIGHT everyone was gathered around the fire, staying warm, with blankets wrapped around them. The electricity was still off, so the room was only lit by the fireplace and candles. It looked beautiful and romantic.

Haley was standing over by the fire. Jeff joined her. "Not exactly the rehearsal dinner we were planning," Jeff said. "But, I have to admit, Steve, you did a great job with what we had. How did you know that about the freezer and when did you learn how to cook? The only thing you used to make in college was mac and cheese from the box."

Steve laughed. "Luckily, I've picked up a thing or two in all my travels."

Kathy was sitting next to Steve on the couch. She looked impressed. "Those goat cheese balls you made with the chopped walnuts and parsley were great."

"And so were those hummus cucumber rolls," Gail said.

Steve held out his hands. "I take tips."

Everyone laughed.

"But I can't really take the credit. The appetizer recipes were Laura's," Steve said. "She calls the goat cheese balls her *Christmas Camp Goat Cheese Delights*, and I agree, they're great and so easy to make, luckily. And I have to give credit to Trisha and Gail for putting together a great spinach apple salad. I think we all pitched in and made a great team."

Gail laughed. "Using flashlights and candles to see with."

"I have to get you some of those electric lanterns for emergencies like this," Jeff said.

"It's a good idea," Ben agreed. "We've just so rarely ever had the power go out up here. We've been spoiled. And speaking of spoiled . . ." Ben picked up a platter of Christmas cookies and started passing them around. "Who wants dessert?"

"Me!" Jeff said as he took a cookie and got one for Haley, too. "Always my favorite part."

"So, what's on the agenda for tomorrow?" Steve asked.

Everyone looked at Trisha. She was sitting in a chair, trying to get her tablet to work but not having any luck. "So far, nothing. It looks like the power on my tablet died, and I can't recharge without any electricity. Not that it matters, because we're not planning a wedding anymore."

Haley gave Jeff a sad look. He kissed her on the cheek. "At least not for Christmas Eve. But we're definitely getting married."

"Someday," Haley said.

Trisha stood up. "I think I'm going to go upstairs and turn in for the night. Ben, is it okay if I take one of these candles with me?"

Ben shook his head. "It's going to get really cold tonight without any heat. We should all stay down here by the fire." He walked over to a stack of rolled-up sleeping bags. "I got these out for everyone. You'll be toasty warm." He tossed one to Trisha. She looked at it like she'd never slept in a sleeping bag before. When Ben tossed one to Kathy, she, on the other hand, looked excited.

"Fun, just like camping!" Kathy said.

"When have you ever gone camping?" Haley asked her.

Kathy smiled. "I've seen it in the movies. I've always wanted to go."

"I've camped all over the world, and I love it," Steve said. "Fire one of those bags over here, Ben."

Ben laughed as he threw one over to Steve.

Jeff went over and helped his dad hand out the rest. When he tossed a bag to Haley, he winked at her. "I told you this would be an adventure."

Haley couldn't help but laugh.

HOURS LATER, HALEY woke not knowing where she was. When she abruptly sat up in her sleeping bag, she realized she was in the sitting room with the rest of the group, sleeping on the floor by the fire. Max was by her side. He was awake, as well. She looked over at Jeff on the other side of her. He was sleeping peacefully. Looking at him, she felt a rush of pure undeniable love. She gently kissed his cheek.

She saw Ben sleeping on one couch, and Gail sleeping on the other. Trisha was sleeping in a chair. Kathy and Steve were also sleeping next to the fire and next to each other. Even Snowball the cat had come out of hiding and was curled up on the couch with Ben.

Haley shivered. It was getting cold. The fire was almost out. Carefully, quietly, she got up and put several more logs on the fire, and it roared back to life. She quickly ran back over to her sleeping bag and snuggled up inside. She looked over at Max, who was watching her. When he put his head down on her chest, she cuddled up with him before closing her eyes and falling back to sleep.

Chapter Nine

HALEY WOKE UP early the next morning to Max licking her face.

"What are you doing?" she whispered as she sat up. Max dropped his leash in front of her and wagged his tail and ran toward the front door. "Are you crazy?" she whispered to him. She looked around, and everyone was still sleeping. "We can't go out there. There's too much snow."

But when Max started circling and looked like he was about to bark, Haley jumped up and put her finger in front of her lips. "Shhhhhh," she whispered. "Everyone's sleeping. Okay, I'll take you out quickly. Just don't bark."

She quickly grabbed Jeff's big snow coat and his boots out of the closet and put on his hat and scarf and put the leash on Max. "I can't believe you're making me go out here in this snowstorm. This was supposed to be my wedding day. You should take pity on me."

Max wagged his tail and waited for her to open the front door. When she did, she was stunned. It wasn't snowing anymore. The sun was just starting to come up, and there wasn't a cloud in the sky.

"Whoa, what happened to the storm?"

For an answer, Max pulled her forward, and she had to run to keep up with him as he started playing in the fresh snow. Haley laughed. He was hilarious. He would bite the snow and jump and then bite the snow again. She made a snowball and threw it at him. He instantly devoured it. She was laughing again when a snowball hit her on the back.

"Hey!" She whirled around and found Jeff walking toward her. She laughed. "What are you doing?"

"Sticking up for Max. I saw you throw that snowball at him." Jeff joined her and kissed her. "Good morning." He shivered. He wasn't wearing a coat.

"Oh no, I stole your coat," Haley laughed. "I'm sorry." She took off his scarf and wrapped it around his neck.

He laughed and looked up at the sky. "It's warmed up a lot."

"I know," Haley said. "What happened to the storm?"

"It's gone."

"But it's still cold and you don't have a coat," Haley said. "Let's get you inside."

Before they got to the door, it opened and Trisha was standing there. "Haley! Jeff! Get in here."

"What's wrong?" Haley asked as she and Jeff hurried toward the door. As soon as they were inside, they saw everyone was up in the sitting room, rolling up their sleeping bags.

"Nothing's wrong," Trisha said. "Everything's finally right. Ben just got a call. Because the storm has passed and the snowplows are already out, they're going to reopen Alpine Road."

Ben and Gail joined them. "That means . . ."

"We have a wedding plan!" Trisha said.

"What?" Haley looked at Jeff. Her eyes were full of hope. "Really?"

"Really," Gail said. "Ben's been calling everyone, and they're all coming."

Haley gave Jeff an incredulous look. "So we can really get married. Tonight . . ."

"On Christmas Eve, just like we always wanted." When Jeff kissed her, Max barked happily, and even Snowball made an appearance and meowed.

FOR HALEY, THE next few hours flew by like a whirlwind. She still couldn't believe the storm was gone, and it was a perfect sunny winter day. It was her wedding day. It was really happening.

Laura had even surprised them all by showing up with her husband on a snowmobile. He dropped her off and said he'd be back with the car once the road reopened. Laura told them she didn't want to miss anything. And now it was such a beautiful day, it had been perfect for a snowmobile trip.

Haley smiled, thinking about how Laura was already in the kitchen working away with Gail. After she'd heard about Steve's success the night before, she had recruited him to help as well, while they waited for Haley's mom to bring the rest of the ingredients. Since they only had a few hours to get everything ready, the original menu wasn't going to work anymore, but Laura had assured Haley there were still enough things they could make that would be wonderful.

Haley had assured them that whatever they made, she knew it would be special, because it had been made with love.

As soon as they knew the wedding was back on, Trisha gathered everyone together and started handing out assignments. Haley had to admit it was impressive how quickly Trisha could shift gears and make things happen. There was no doubt she was a great wedding planner and everyone respected that, including Haley.

The guys were assigned to go get the Douglas fir branches they hadn't been able to get the night before because of the storm. As soon as they got back, Trisha started showing Haley and Kathy how to put together a beautiful arrangement using all the things from the flower shop, including the white roses. Haley couldn't believe how incredible they turned out.

As the sun started to go down, Haley kept looking out the window, excited for people to start arriving. But

Trisha was firm, insisting that Haley wait until after the ceremony to see everyone, so she had time to get ready and could make a grand entrance.

Haley didn't care at all about making a grand entrance, but when she saw how hard Trisha was working to make the day special, she agreed to do what Trisha asked. Trisha had even had the photographer, Curt, bring along his sister, who specialized in doing hair and makeup. Haley agreed to stay upstairs and wait to see everyone.

Kathy had also pointed out it was bad luck to see the groom before the wedding, and with the way this wedding had gone, they all agreed they didn't want to take that chance and jinx anything.

At least Trisha had let Haley's mom and dad come up to see her, and they were all able to catch up while Haley was getting her hair and makeup done. Curt captured everything, getting some wonderful family candid shots that Haley's mom was already raving about.

Everything, dare she even think it, was going wonderfully.

The last thing for Haley to do was put on Jeff's mom's wedding dress. Her own mom and Kathy helped her, as Curt took more pictures. It was a beautiful moment, and at one point, all three of them were crying. Trisha had instantly appeared with tissues for each of them. Trisha stood back admiring Haley in the dress. "The dress is beautiful on you," she said, smiling a genuine smile. "Grace was a very special person. She was always like another mom to me. She was so kind and loving . . ." When Trisha's voice got choked up with emotion and trailed off, Haley looked over and saw Trisha was holding back tears. She was surprised. It was the first time Haley thought about the fact that Trisha had known Grace and she had lost Grace, too. Her heart went out to her. She took Trisha's hand. "You have done a beautiful job with this wedding, and I'm sure Grace is so thankful that you've done all this for Jeff and for Ben. That you were here when she couldn't be."

When Trisha's eyes filled with tears, Haley handed her a tissue.

They smiled at each other—a real smile, for the first time.

"Thank you for saying that," Trisha said. "I miss her very much, and Jeff and Ben, they've been like my family. I've missed them, too, these last few years." Trisha wiped her tears and pulled herself together. "I'm sorry for the way I acted when we met. I really do love Jeff, but I've realized, watching you two, we never had what you have, and what I really loved was being part of this family. I can see how much Jeff loves you, and Ben, too. You make them happy and that's all I want."

Haley, touched, reached out and took Trisha's hand. "Thank you." She was starting to tear up, too.

As soon as Trisha saw that, she went right back into wedding planner mode.

"Don't you even think about crying," Trisha said. "You'll ruin your makeup."

Haley laughed. Trisha gave her a stern look, then after a moment, laughed with her. "Okay, let's do this wedding," Trisha said. "Before something else goes wrong."

Haley laughed again. "Don't even say that!"

Trisha headed for the bedroom door. "I'm going to go check downstairs to make sure everything is ready. We should be getting started in seven minutes."

After Trisha left the room, Haley looked down and saw both Max and Snowball looking up at her.

"I'm about to officially become part of your family. I hope you guys are okay with that?"

Haley laughed when Max barked and wagged his tail. She decided to take that as a yes. As she slowly walked over and looked at her reflection in the mirror, she smiled and took a deep breath. With her eyes closed, she whispered softly, "I promise I will love and take care of your son, Jeff and Ben, always." She opened her eyes just as Kathy came into the room.

Kathy looked stunning in her burgundy velvet cocktail dress. She twirled around in front of Haley. "I'm so glad I kept this dress."

Haley smiled at her. "And it looks amazing on you. You're glowing, but I don't think it's just from the dress . . ."

Kathy couldn't stop smiling. Excited, she took Haley's hand. "It's Steve. I know you said not to get carried away, but I honestly think he might be the one to give me a chance at my own HEA, my happily ever after."

"You know there's nothing I want more for you,"

Haley said. "He seems to really like you, too. This could be the start of something really special."

Kathy shook her head. "I'm sorry. Look at me going on and on when today is about you. I think I just feel so much love all around me here, with you and Jeff and Ben and Gail. It's really beautiful, and speaking of beautiful, I don't know how all this worked out so well but you are truly one of the most beautiful brides I've ever seen. I am so happy for you. I love you, and I love Jeff." Kathy walked over and picked up Haley's bridal bouquet that was on the dresser. It looked magical. "This turned out so well. Wait, you added a pinecone . . ."

Haley smiled. "I did. It's a Christmas tradition in Jeff's family and now mine, too. When Jeff's dad proposed to his mom he put the ring in a pinecone and proposed up at Star Peak. Ever since, it has been a tradition in Jeff's family to go up to Star Peak every Christmas and get a pinecone to make a Christmas wish. Then you bring the pinecone back to the inn and put it in that basket of pinecones by the fire, with all the other Christmas wishes."

Kathy smiled. "I saw that basket! I love this."

Haley nodded. "And Jeff proposed to me the same way, up at Star Peak." Haley smiled, looking at the pinecone in her bouquet. "This pinecone is my Christmas wish. I know Jeff will see it and understand."

"Who knew all you needed was a pinecone to make a Christmas wish," Kathy said. "I'm going to go find one immediately."

They shared a laugh.

"Okay, let's make sure you have everything," Kathy said. "Where are your vows?"

Haley touched her heart. "They're right here."

Kathy looked concerned. "You don't have a copy written down?"

"I never got a chance," Haley said, "but that's okay. It doesn't have to be perfect. I know what I want to say. I don't need to write anything down."

Kathy smiled at her. "I knew you would figure it out. Okay, next. Making sure we have something borrowed—the dress that also counts for something old. You have the pinecone—that's something new—but what about something blue? Wait, we forgot something blue!"

Haley reached out and took Kathy's hand. "It's okay. Don't worry about it. We don't need it."

"What?" Kathy gave her an incredulous look. "Yes, we do. We are not taking any more chances jinxing this wedding."

Trisha walked in smiling. "Don't worry. There will be no more jinxing." She held up a pretty white lace garter with a tiny blue bow.

Haley laughed. "No. That's so old school. I don't need that . . ."

Trisha and Kathy interrupted at the same time. "Yes, you do!"

Trisha gave it to Haley. "Keep it. I have plenty. It's part of the wedding planner emergency kit I always have with me."

"Wow, okay, if you both insist," Haley said.

"We do," Trisha said. "And it's time to get started. Are you ready?"

Haley quickly slipped on the something blue and nodded. She knew, without a doubt, she was 100 percent ready.

Chapter Ten

RIGHT AS HALEY was about to leave her room, her dad appeared. He looked so handsome in his black suit and burgundy tie. He smiled when he saw her.

"There's my beautiful girl," he said and took both her hands. "I just wanted to check in on you one more time to make sure you're ready." He kissed her hands.

Haley looked into his eyes. "I am." She smiled. "Do you believe this is really happening, after everything we've been through?"

"I do," he said. "Because when two people love each other as much as you and Jeff do, you're meant to be together. Nothing can stop you. Not a flood, or a snow-storm, nothing."

Haley kissed her dad on the cheek. "Thanks, Dad. You know, I started to get scared, but then I remembered what you'd always say about you and mom when times were tough . . ."

"That true loves only gets stronger during the tough times . . ."

"And better," Haley finished for him. "Because I love him with my whole heart."

"That's my girl. You know your mom and I have been talking, and we talked to Ben, and we've decided that we're going to do a Christmas Camp at the B&B. We saw how much coming here helped you and we want to be able to create that same kind of experience for our guests. This is just the beginning for all of us and I just wanted to tell you how much your mom and I love you and how happy we are for you."

Haley nodded. For a moment she was too emotional to say anything, but as he left she called after him. "I love you both so much."

Haley took a deep breath, as she waited in her room alone. She knew that when the Christmas song *Have Yourself a Merry Little Christmas* started playing that was her cue to start walking down the stairs where everyone would be gathered below waiting for her. The fact that it was Christmas Eve and that she would be walking down the same stairs she had walked down a year ago, when she had reluctantly come to Christmas Camp for the first time, never dreaming how much her life would change, felt like the perfect start to her own happily ever after.

Over the last year, by opening up her heart for the first time, she had experienced so much joy and love and laughter, and she couldn't wait to start her new life with Jeff.

When she heard her cue she took a deep breath and looked around at all the angels in the room, she smiled. She felt so grateful for the journey she'd been on, even with all the ups and downs, because it had brought her here, where she knew she was meant to be. By finally learning how to open her heart and let love in, her entire future had changed. She couldn't wait to marry Jeff and start that future together.

Feeling excited and confident, Haley opened her bedroom door and couldn't help but laugh when she saw Max waiting there for her.

"You are the other love of my life. You know that, right?" Haley said.

Max wagged his tail and walked by her side as she headed for the stairs.

When Haley got to the top of the stairs her smile was radiant. There was a collective "ahhh" when everyone standing below looked up and saw her for the first time.

Haley could feel the love and knew this was the wedding she was meant to have.

As she slowly descended the staircase she looked around and saw all the people from her Christmas Camp—John and his kids, Madison and Blake; and Susie and Ian—she felt so blessed. They had been such a big part of the journey last year when she had redis-covered her Christmas spirit, allowing her to let Jeff into her heart.

Standing next to them was Laura and her husband. Laura wore a pretty black dress with a burgundy shawl. She knew how much Laura loved Jeff and Ben and felt thankful that she now was also included in that love.

The next person she saw was Gail standing next to Ben. She looked beautiful holding little Snowball, who had a burgundy ribbon tied around her neck. Ben looked distinguished and proud in his black suit. He touched his heart and had tears of joy in his eyes when he saw Haley was wearing Jeff's mom's dress.

When Haley looked over to her parents, she also saw tears of happiness in her mom's eyes. When her mom mouthed the words "I love you," Haley whispered, "I love you."

And then there was Jeff, the love of her life, stand-ing there, wearing his tuxedo, looking more handsome than she had ever seen him look. But what really mat-tered most to her was how he was looking back at her. In his eyes, she saw so much genuine love that it made her feel safe and cherished. She knew that together they could handle anything, and she couldn't wait for their own adventure to begin.

When she got to the bottom of the stairs and he took her hand, he looked into her eyes and softly said, "I love you."

She smiled back at him. "I love you, too."

As he led her into the sitting room, she stopped and looked around in awe. The entire ceiling was covered with rows and rows of white twinkling lights. The only other light came from candles and the fireplace. It was magical. Now she knew why Trisha had wanted her to stay upstairs, so they could surprise her.

As Jeff guided her over to the fireplace, where her dad was waiting to officiate the wedding, she looked up at him and whispered, "It's beautiful."

THE CEREMONY WAS equally beautiful. Haley and Jeff recited their own vows that had people laughing and crying all at the same time. It was a true celebration of their love. After the ceremony, Trisha orchestrated the picture taking, making sure everyone got a special picture with Haley and Jeff. The whole time, Haley was in a daze of happiness. She kept looking at her wedding ring and at Jeff, making sure it all wasn't just a dream, that this was real. She still couldn't believe she was married to someone who loved her and that she loved with all her heart.

They had just finished taking a picture with John, Madison, and Blake, when Trisha ushered them into the dining room to get a picture with the wedding cake.

Haley looked confused. "But we didn't make a cake. We didn't have time."

Trisha, looking stern, walked up to Haley. "Any wedding I organize has a cake." When Trisha moved out of the way, Haley gasped.

On the dining room table was her dream wedding cake. Just like the one that was destroyed at her parents'. Only instead of six different snow-white tiers, there were three smaller tiers, all in the shape of different squares so it looked like a bundle of Christmas presents all wrapped up with a pretty burgundy fondant bow.

Stunned, she looked at Jeff. "How did you do this?" She wiped tears from her eyes. "You know how much this meant to me."

Jeff kissed her cheek. "I didn't. Trisha did."

Haley spun around to look at Trisha. "What? How?"

"Kathy showed me the picture on your phone and told me what happened . . ."

Haley looked from Trisha to Kathy.

Trisha continued. "I called in a favor with a pastry chef I know, a big favor because they pretty much worked around the clock to make it happen, and I had Gail pick it up and bring it here. I wanted it to be a surprise."

Incredulous, Haley walked over to Trisha and took her hand. "Thank you. This means so much to me."

Trisha smiled a genuine smile. "I'm glad I could do it for you."

When Haley hugged Trisha, Jeff and Ben came over and hugged her, as well.

"Thank you, Trisha," Jeff said. "For everything."

Trisha smiled back at him and at Haley. "You're welcome."

Jeff picked up the cake knife. "Okay, who wants cake?"

Haley, laughing, took the knife from him. "We haven't even had dinner yet . . ."

Jeff smiled and gave her a confused look. "So?"

Haley laughed and kissed him. "I love you so much."

When they kissed, the photographer got the perfect shot. In the picture, you see Haley and Jeff kissing, and in the background, there's Ben and Gail, also looking very much in love, and Kathy and Steve holding hands, and you know another Christmas Camp love story is about to begin . . .

So you can re-create your own Christmas Camp Wedding greenery arrangements, here are some of the ideas that Haley used for her wedding at the Holly Peak Inn.

Christmas Camp
Wedding Greenery Arrangement

Materials Needed:

1 14–16 inch wicker basket (with waterproof liner)
   or decorative container
1 floral foam (make sure it is for fresh flowers) and
   a tray for water

Wire wooded pegs to anchor pinecones
Douglas fir branches cut 12–14 inches long
4–6 holly branches with bright red berries
4–6 flowers of choice (Haley used white roses.
    Red carnations also last a long time.)
Several pinecones for your own Christmas wishes

Please adjust the amount of materials based on the size of the arrangement you would like. These approximate numbers are based on a basket 14–16 inches wide. The amount of branches you will use will depend on the fullness of each branch.

Additional Decorative Ideas:

Additional evergreens, like Balsam fir,
    if wanted for variety
Small red ornaments to hang on branches
Burlap or red velvet ribbon for a bow

Directions:

1. Cut all stems at an angle and soak in water for a half hour before creating.
2. Soak floral foam all the way through, put on tray and into lined basket.
3. Start by putting the Douglas fir branches into the foam, horizontally, all around the bottom, then

adding diagonally and vertically in the middle, doing the top last. The goal is not to see the foam.

4. Next, disperse the holly branches all around the basket.
5. Add flowers (be sure to strip flowers of all thorns and leaves, just leaving the stem).
6. Attach pinecones to wooden pegs and add to the arrangement. Make your wish!

Tips:

1. Make sure tray always has water and store in a cool place away from the sun.
2. Mist lightly every few days with water and trade out flowers if needed.

Here's Laura's recipe for an easy delicious party appetizer you can whip up in no time, even if the power goes out!

Christmas Camp
Goat Cheese Delights Recipe

Prep time: 10 minutes
Skill Level: Easy
Makes: 20

Ingredients:

1 pound of soft goat cheese
½ cup crushed walnuts
4 tablespoons parsley (flat leaf)
1–2 teaspoons black pepper (optional)
Honey to drizzle on top (optional)

Directions:

1. Combine crushed walnuts and parsley in medium bowl and set aside.
2. Combine soft goat cheese with pepper.
3. Use goat cheese to make 20 small bite-sized balls.
4. Roll balls in the walnut/parsley mix until generously covered.
5. Drizzle with honey (optional).
6. Eat immediately or refrigerate until ready to serve. Serve at room temperature.
7. Serve with crackers and bread or eat alone.

Optional Ingredients:

Cranberries
Pecans
Pistachios
Rosemary
Thyme

Acknowledgments

I GREW UP watching and loving Lifetime and Hallmark Christmas movies where most of the couples didn't declare their love or kiss until the very end of the movie. It always left me wondering, what happened after that kiss? Did they really get their Happily Ever After? Did they go on and date, get married, have a family? I wanted to know what happened next.

So when I wrote my TV movie *Christmas Camp* I decided to also write the *Christmas Camp* novel and sequel *Christmas Camp Wedding*, so everyone could continue the journey with Haley and Jeff and find out what happened after their kiss.

To do the TV movie and both book projects in the same tight timeline wouldn't have been possible without the support and encouragement from my steadfast entertainment attorney Neville Johnson, my always encouraging Foundry + Media literary agent, Jessica Regel, and the truly talented and enthusiastic HarperCollins publishing team lead by Liate Stehlik and Jennifer Hart and my editor, May Chen.

From the moment I met May at HarperCollins, I am very thankful to say my publishing collaboration has been one of the most positive experiences in my career. I would also like to stay a heartfelt thank-you to associate editor Elle Keck, copy editor Anne Sharpe, Amelia Wood in marketing, publicist Pamela Spengler Jaffee, and cover artist Amy Halperin.

Before I send in the first draft of any manuscript, I'm truly blessed to have my mom, Lao Schaler, and bonus mom, Kathy Bezold, read everything I write and give priceless feedback, and my ingenious friend Heather Mikesell copyedit so I can write like the wind and make all my tight deadlines.

What a journey this has been! I couldn't be more grateful for all the continued love and support from my family, including my dad, Harry Schaler, my grandparents Harry and Betty Schaler, my grandmother, Pat Crane, and the rest of the clan.

And for my treasured friends, Greta, Lee, Clint, Lorianne, Lisa, Amy, Tim, Denise, Delia, Heather, and Jeryl, who are like my family, who hung in there with me even when I basically had to disappear to make the TV movie and two books happen.

And finally, a heartfelt thank-you to you, my dear reader, for taking the time to share in Haley and Jeff's story at *Christmas Camp* and at *Christmas Camp Wedding*. Thank you for also caring about what happened next . . .

About the Author

KAREN SCHALER is a three-time Emmy award–winning storyteller, author, screenwriter, journalist, and national TV host. She has written original screenplays for Netflix, Hallmark, and Lifetime Christmas movies, and is the creator and host of *Travel Therapy TV* and author of *Travel Therapy: Where Do You Need to Go?* Her travels to more than sixty-five countries inspired *Christmas Camp*, the novel and movie. Karen is passionate about telling uplifting and empowering stories that are filled with heart and hope. When she's not traveling, you can find Karen in New York City or visiting her family in Washington State.

Discover great authors, exclusive authors, and more at hc.com.